To

Ben,

Merry Christmas 2002

All Our Love, hugs and kisses,

Uncal Jay, Antie Heather

Jordan, Sammy and Becky

x x x x x
x x x
x

This book belongs to...

B Hastings

Ben Ross Hastings

A
Collection of
Jungle Tales

This is a Parragon Book
This edition published in 2002
Parragon, Queen Street House,
4 Queen Street, Bath BA1 1HE, UK

Copyright © Parragon 2001

Created and produced by
The Complete Works

ISBN 0-75258-608-4

Printed in China

A Collection of Jungle Tales

Written by Ronne Randall
Illustrated by Jacqueline East

Contents

monkey mayhem!

Written by Ronne Randall
Illustrated by Jacqueline East

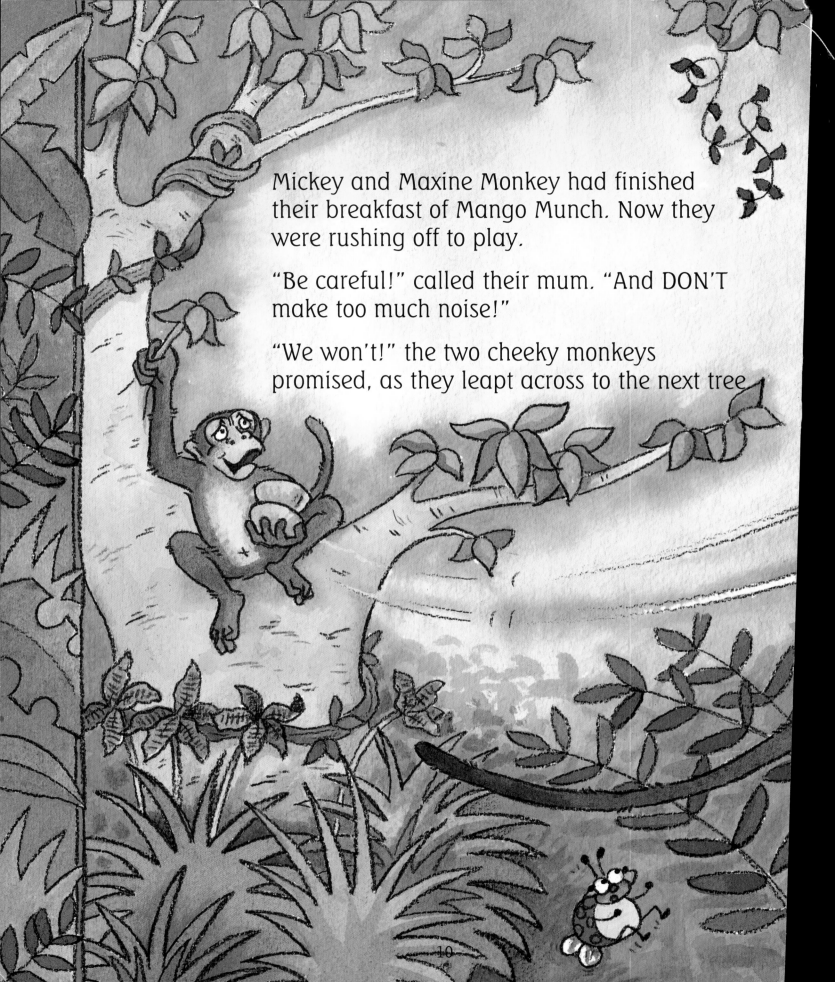

Mickey and Maxine Monkey had finished their breakfast of Mango Munch. Now they were rushing off to play.

"Be careful!" called their mum. "And DON'T make too much noise!"

"We won't!" the two cheeky monkeys promised, as they leapt across to the next tree

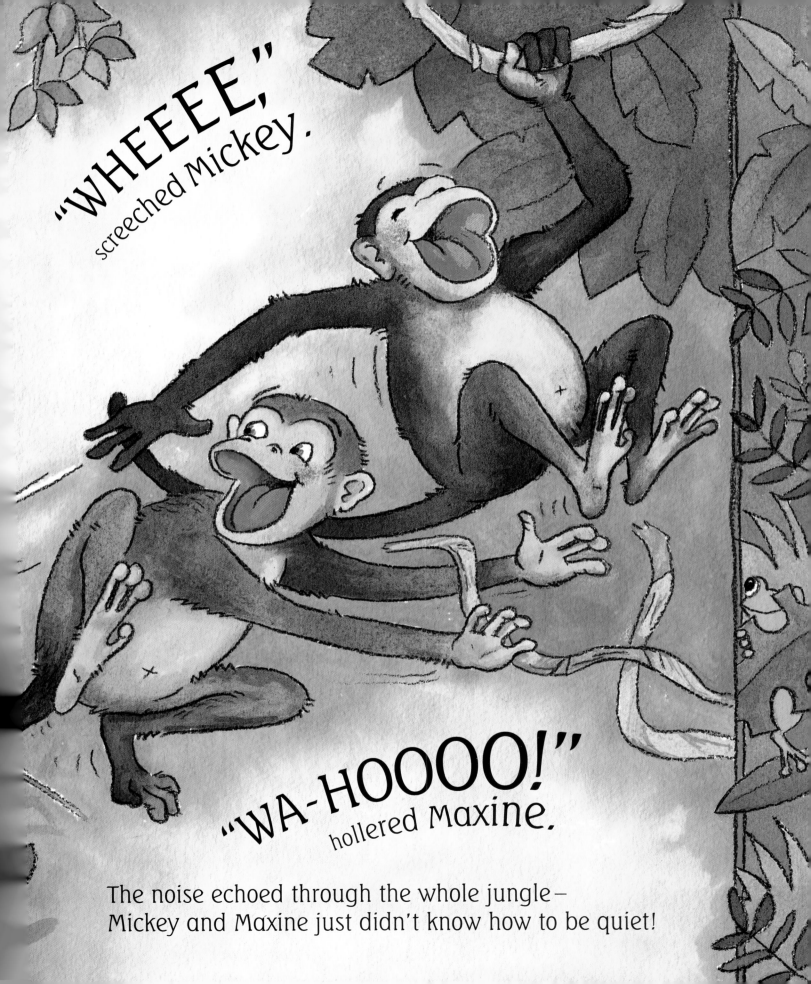

"WHEEE," screeched Mickey.

"WA-HOOOO!" hollered Maxine.

The noise echoed through the whole jungle—
Mickey and Maxine just didn't know how to be quiet!

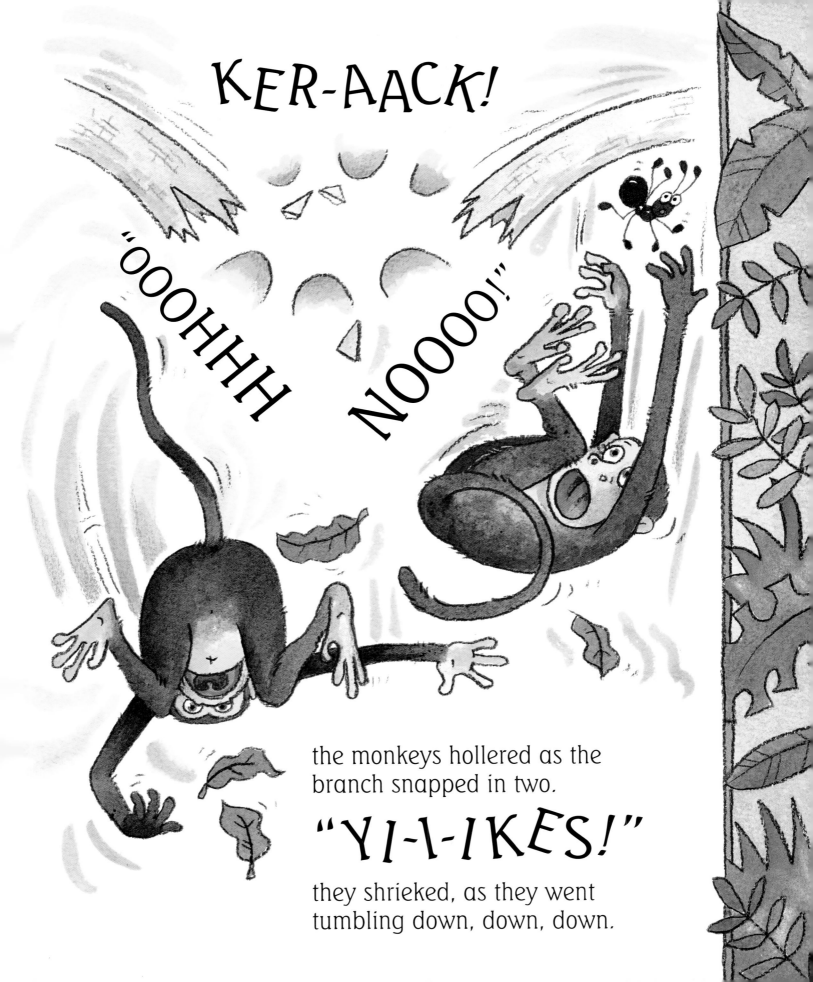

the monkeys hollered as the branch snapped in two.

they shrieked, as they went tumbling down, down, down.

KER-THUMMPPP!
SPROI-OI-OING!

The jungle shook as the two monkeys crashed to the ground, then sprang to their feet.

"YIPPPEEEEEE!" the monkeys cheered, brushing themselves off.

"That was so much FUN!" exclaimed Maxine. "Let's go get Chico Chimp and see if he wants to do it, too!"

Chattering as they went, the two monkeys scrambled back up to the tree tops.

"HEY, CHICO! COME AND PLAY WITH US!" they bellowed as they swung through the branches towards the chimps' house.

All through the jungle, animals shook their heads and covered their ears. Couldn't anyone keep those naughty, noisy monkeys quiet?

Chico Chimp was soon ready to play with his friends. The three of them had a great time swinging, tumbling, and bouncing together. Then they spotted a coconut palm.

"Hey!" shouted Chico. "Let's get some coconuts!"

"Great!" said Maxine. "Last one up the tree
is a rotten banana!"

But before they got to the coconut palm, they stopped short. Grandpa Gorilla was standing in their path, glaring at them angrily.

"**Clear off**, you mischief-makers," he said. "You've given everyone enough headaches for one day. My grandson Gulliver is fast asleep down by the river, and if you wake him up, I will be very, very upset!"

"Sorry," whispered Maxine, looking down at the ground. Everyone in the jungle knew it was a big mistake to upset Grandpa Gorilla!

"We'll be quiet," the three friends promised.

Mickey, Maxine and Chico slowly wandered away. As they got nearer to the coconut palm, Mickey said, "Let's just climb the tree. We can do that quietly."

"Okay," the others agreed half-heartedly.

"I suppose it's better than doing nothing," said Maxine.

From their perch up among the coconuts, the three friends could see what was happening all over the jungle.

They saw Jerome Giraffe showing his son Jeremy how to choose the juiciest, most tender leaves on a tree...

...and they saw Portia Parrot giving her daughter Penelope her first flying lesson.

And right below them, they saw little Gulliver Gorilla sleeping contentedly in the tall grass beside the river.

And – uh-oh! They saw something else, too. Claudia Crocodile was in the river. She was grinning and snapping her big, sharp teeth – and heading straight for Gulliver!

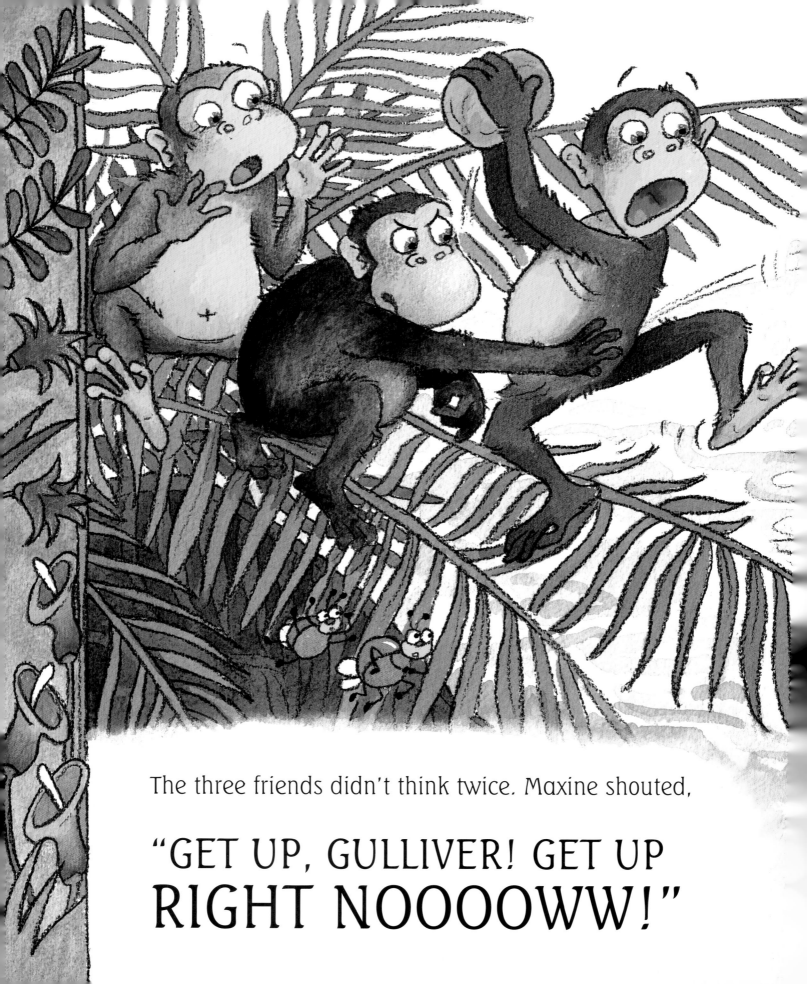

The three friends didn't think twice. Maxine shouted,

"GET UP, GULLIVER! GET UP RIGHT NOOOOWW!"

At the same time, Mickey and Chico began throwing coconuts at Claudia.

SMAACCCKK!

THWAACKK!
went the coconuts.

they went, right on Claudia's hard crocodile head.

"OWW-WOOWW"
moaned Claudia.

"OWW-WOW OWW-WOW!"

"What's going on here?" Grandpa Gorilla shouted up into the coconut tree. "I thought I told you three to keep quiet!"

28

All the noise woke Gulliver. The little gorilla sat up, looked around, and ran to his grandpa, who was hurrying towards the river.

Then he saw Claudia swimming away, and he realised what had happened. He grabbed Gulliver and gave him a great big gorilla hug. "I'm so glad you're safe!" he said.

Maxine, Mickey and Chico came down from the tree.

"We're sorry we made so much noise," Chico said.

By this time all the other gorillas had gathered round, and so had most of the other jungle animals.

"What's all the commotion about?"
asked Jerome Giraffe.

"Yes, what's going on?" squawked
Portia Parrot.

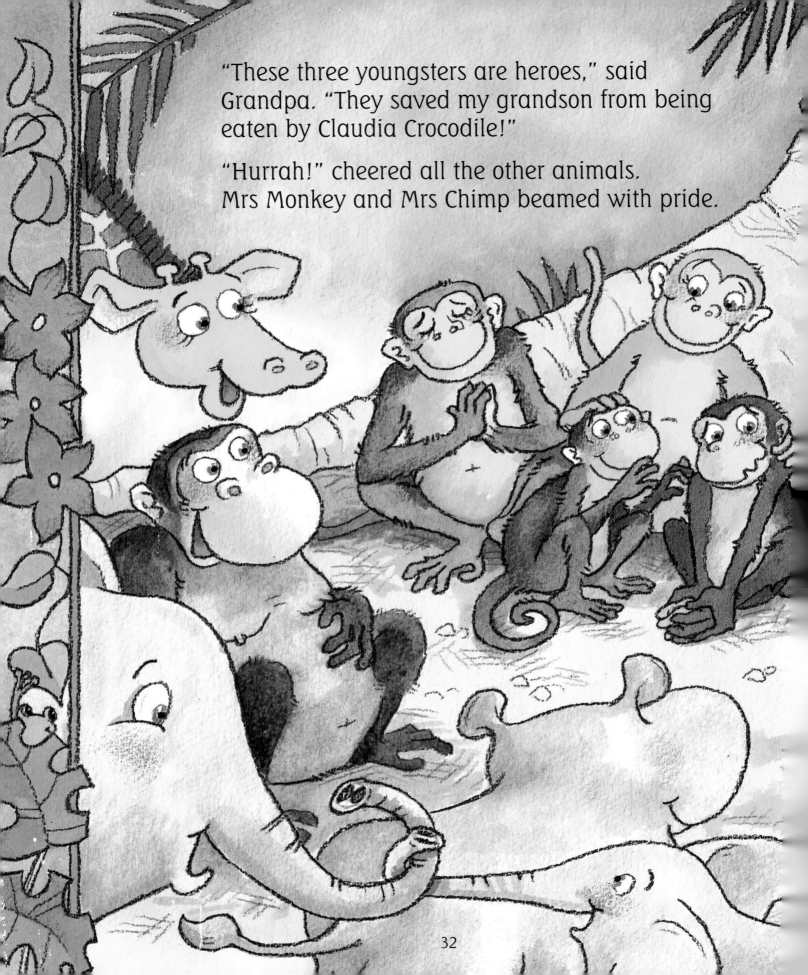

"These three youngsters are heroes," said Grandpa. "They saved my grandson from being eaten by Claudia Crocodile!"

"Hurrah!" cheered all the other animals. Mrs Monkey and Mrs Chimp beamed with pride.

32

"I think you deserve a reward,"
said Grandpa Gorilla. "And I think
your reward should be…"

All the other animals held their breath in anticipation.

33

PEEEEE!"

cheered Mickey, Maxine and Chico, in their loudest, screechiest voices. Their grins were almost as wide as the river.

"OH, NOOOOOOO!"

all the other animals groaned together – but they were all smiling, too.

The End

trunk
trouble

Written by Ronne Randall
Illustrated by Jacqueline East

Emma, Ellen and Eric Elephant had spent nearly all day at the river, splashing and sploshing in the cool, clear water and giving each other excellent elephant showers.

But now it was nearly dinner time, and their rumbling tummies told them it was time to head for home.

First the little elephants had to dry themselves off.
They made their way out to the clearing, and
carefully dusted themselves with fine earth and sand.

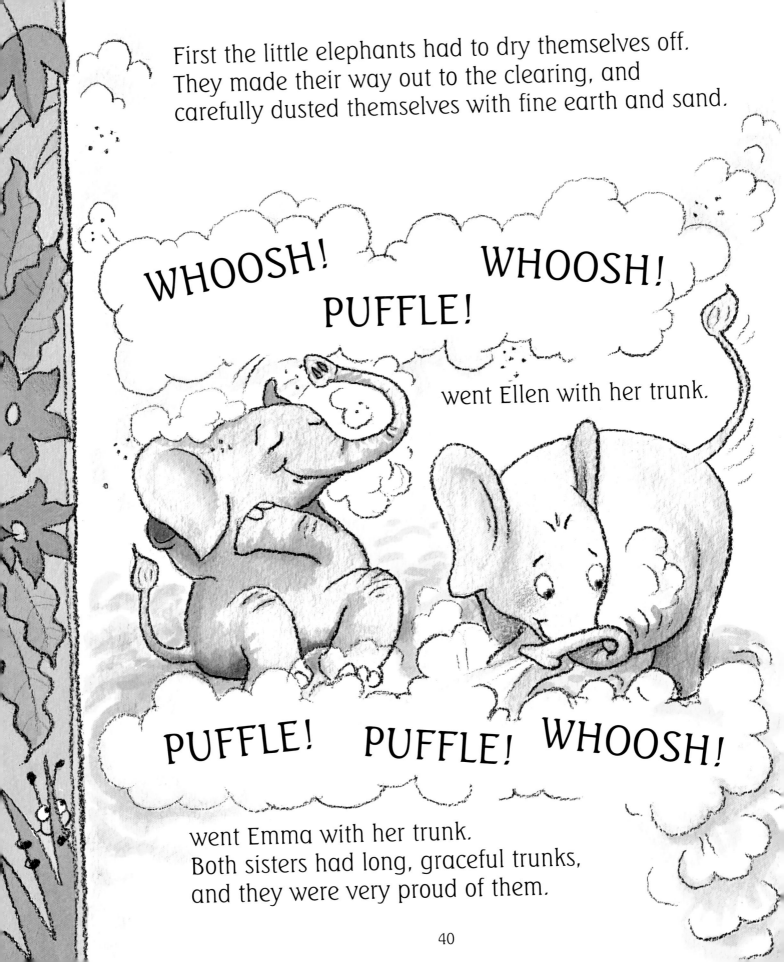

WHOOSH!   WHOOSH!
PUFFLE!

went Ellen with her trunk.

PUFFLE!   PUFFLE!   WHOOSH!

went Emma with her trunk.
Both sisters had long, graceful trunks,
and they were very proud of them.

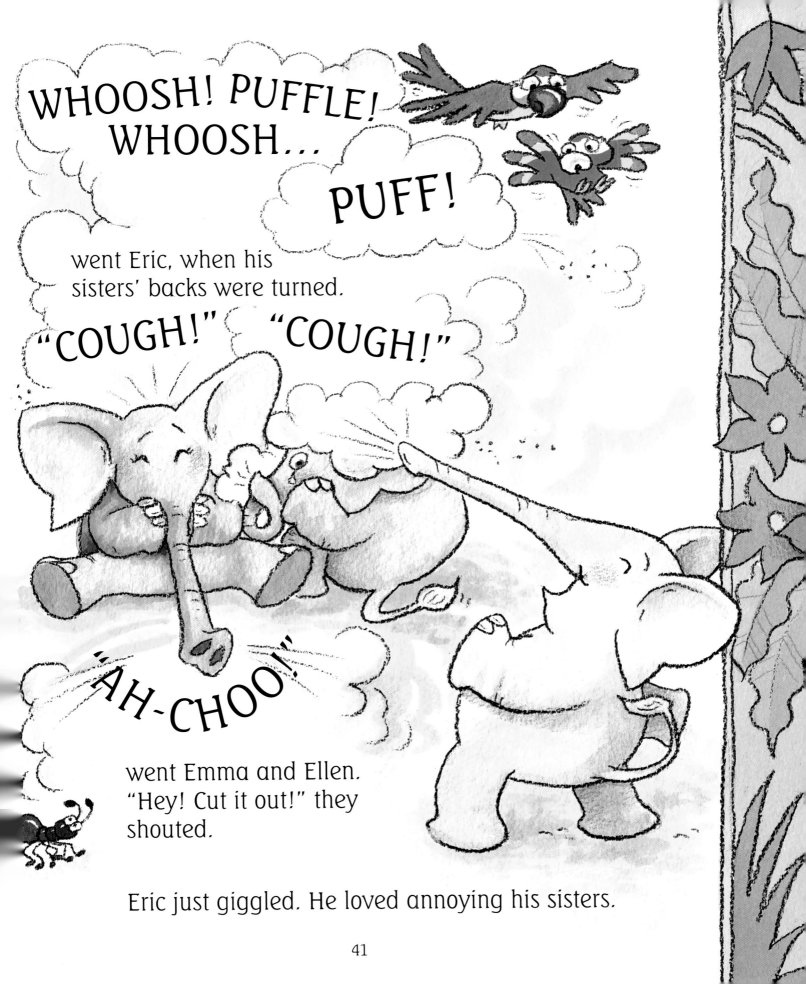

WHOOSH! PUFFLE! WHOOSH...
PUFF!

went Eric, when his sisters' backs were turned.

"COUGH!" "COUGH!"

"AH-CHOO!"

went Emma and Ellen. "Hey! Cut it out!" they shouted.

Eric just giggled. He loved annoying his sisters.

"I'll race you home!" Eric called, when they were all dry. "Last one back is an elephant egg!" And he loped back into the jungle.

Ellen and Emma ran after him. "We'll get there first! We'll beat you!" they cried, going as quickly as they could.

Ellen and Emma were running so fast and trying so hard to catch up with their brother that they forgot to look where they were going.

All at once, Emma's feet got caught in a leafy, trailing vine, and she stumbled and lost her balance.

"Oh-oh-OOOOHHHH!" she cried as she slipped and staggered and started to fall.

"Grab my trunk!" Ellen cried, reaching out to her sister.

But Emma grabbed her sister's trunk so hard that she pulled Ellen down with her. As the two elephants struggled to straighten up, their trunks got twisted together in a great big tangle.

"Help!" they cried. "Eric! Help!"

When their brother turned and saw what had happened, he came bounding back.

"Don't worry!" he called. "I'll save you!"

Eric reached out with his trunk to try to help his sisters up. But the vine leaves were very slippery, and as he grabbed his sisters' trunks, he slipped and lost his balance, too. Now Eric's trunk was all tangled up with Emma's and Ellen's!

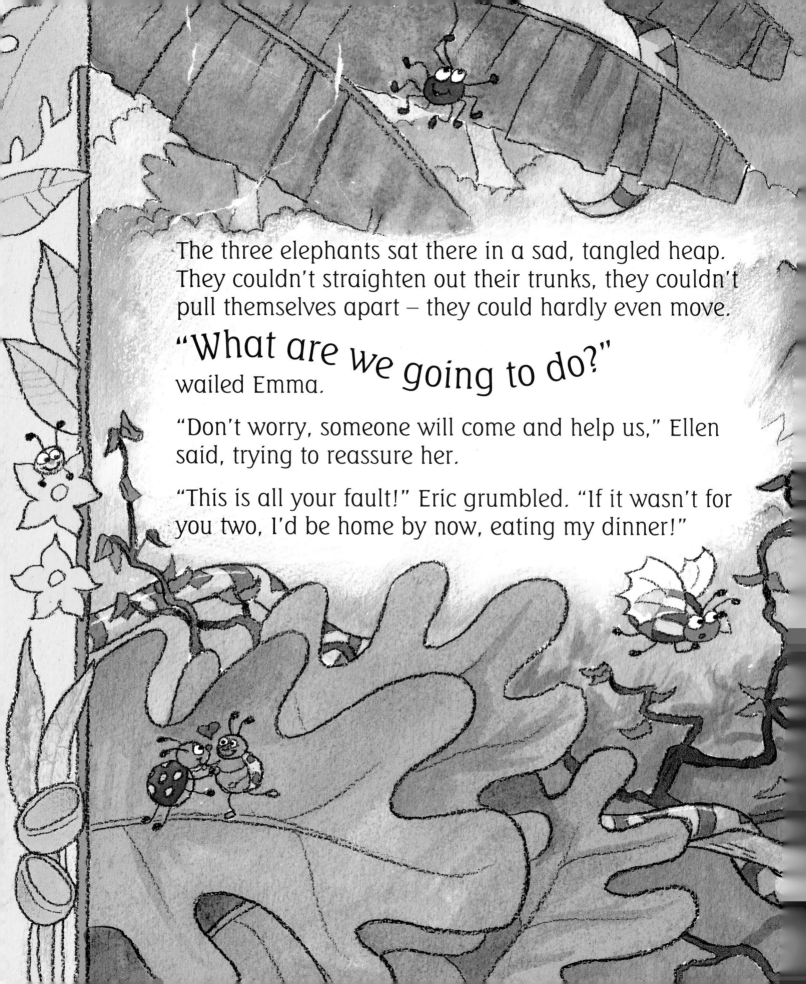

The three elephants sat there in a sad, tangled heap. They couldn't straighten out their trunks, they couldn't pull themselves apart – they could hardly even move.

"What are we going to do?" wailed Emma.

"Don't worry, someone will come and help us," Ellen said, trying to reassure her.

"This is all your fault!" Eric grumbled. "If it wasn't for you two, I'd be home by now, eating my dinner!"

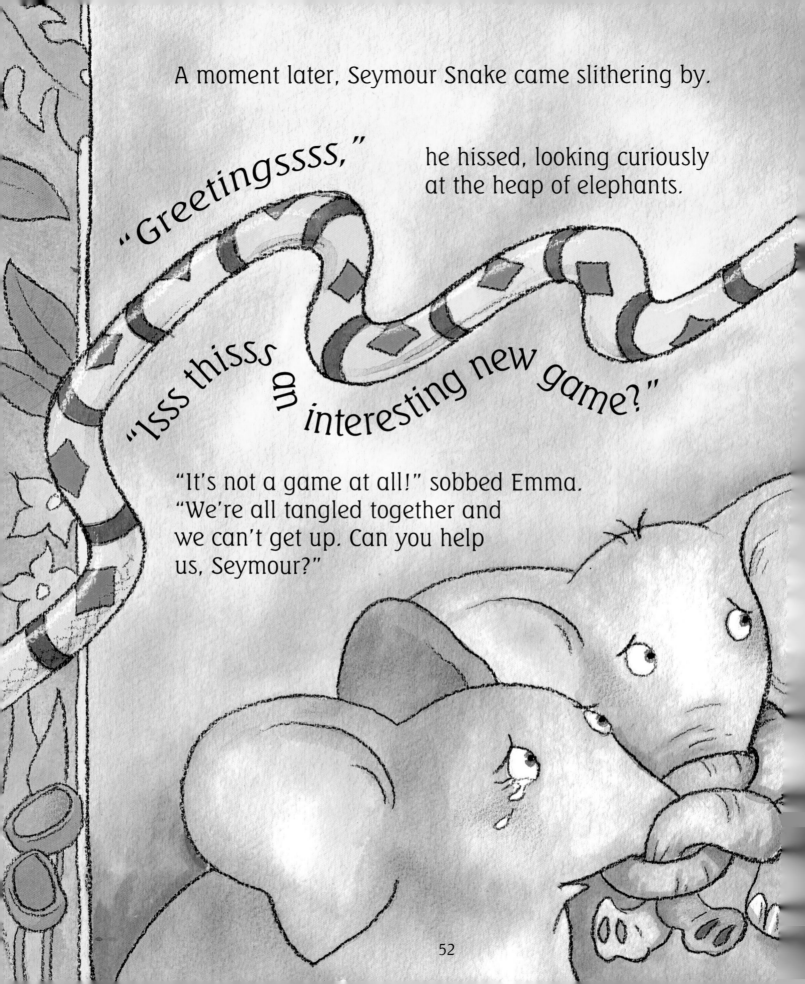

A moment later, Seymour Snake came slithering by.

"Greetingssss," he hissed, looking curiously at the heap of elephants.

"Isss thisss an interesting new game?"

"It's not a game at all!" sobbed Emma. "We're all tangled together and we can't get up. Can you help us, Seymour?"

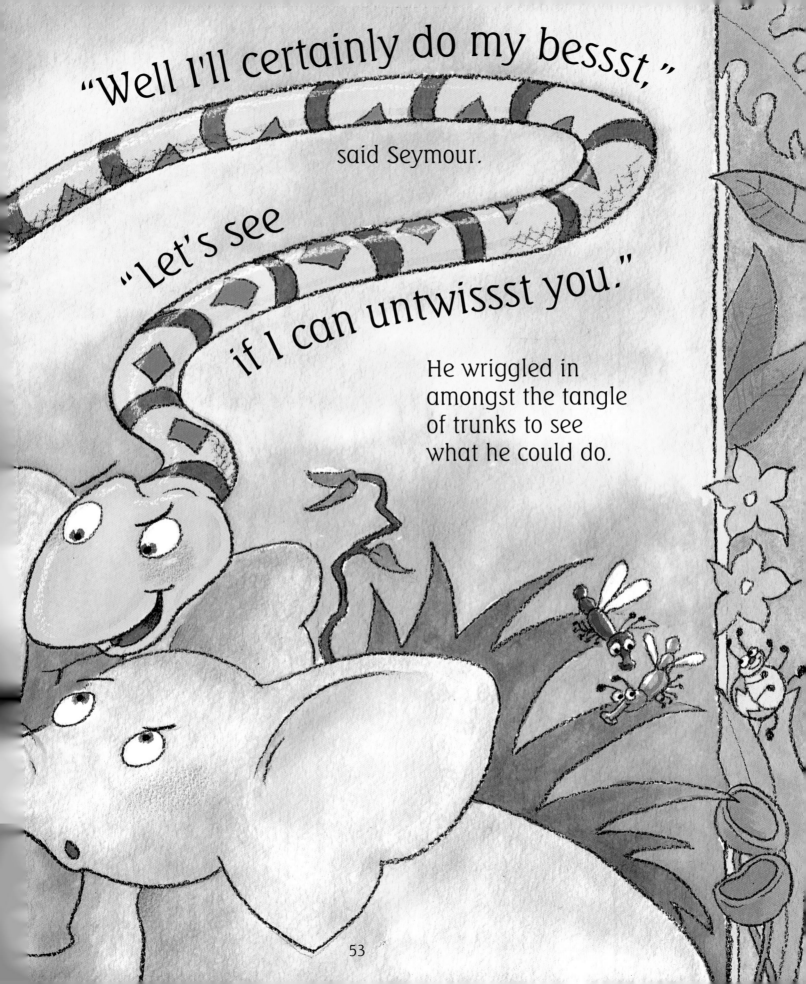

"Well I'll certainly do my bessst,"

said Seymour.

"Let's see

if I can untwissst you."

He wriggled in amongst the tangle of trunks to see what he could do.

53

But everything was so muddled and jumbled together that Seymour couldn't even find his way out!

"Graciousss me!

he exclaimed.

"I ssseem to be sssstuck!"

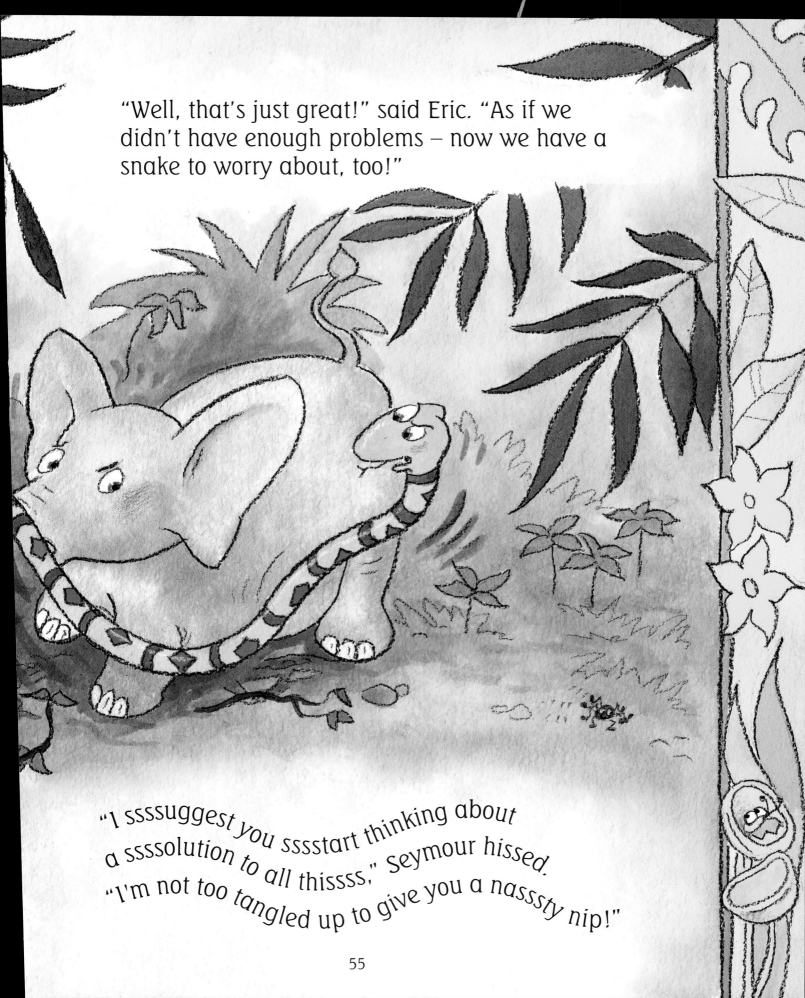

"Well, that's just great!" said Eric. "As if we didn't have enough problems – now we have a snake to worry about, too!"

"I ssssuggest you sssstart thinking about a ssssolution to all thissss," Seymour hissed. "I'm not too tangled up to give you a nasssty nip!"

Just then Mickey and Maxine Monkey came swinging
through the branches.

"HEY, YOU GUYS!"

they shouted. They weren't very far
away – Mickey and Maxine always
shouted.

"WHAT'S
GOING ON?"

"We're stuck!" cried Ellen. "Please help us get untangled so we can go home!"

"Well, we can try pulling you apart," said Maxine, scurrying down to inspect the pile of elephants and snake. "Mickey, you take a tail, and I'll take some ears."

57

Mickey grabbed hold of Eric's tail, and Maxine gripped Ellen's ears. Then they both pulled and pulled and

p-u-l-l-e-d.

"OUCH!"
cried Eric.

"OUCH-OUCH-OOUUCCHH!"
bellowed Ellen.

"I'm being ssssqueezzzzed breathlessssss!" hissed Seymour in alarm.

Mickey and Maxine gave up. Pulling clearly wasn't going to work.

Suddenly there was a flapping up above as Portia Parrot and her daughter Penelope landed in a tree. They had something in their beaks, and as everyone looked up, they let it go. A large cloud of dry, dusty, sandy earth drifted down.

"Cough-cough-ca-choooo!"

spluttered Mickey and Maxine.

"Cough-cough-ca-choooo!"

thundered the elephants.

For a moment, they didn't know what had happened. Then they realised – they had sneezed themselves apart!

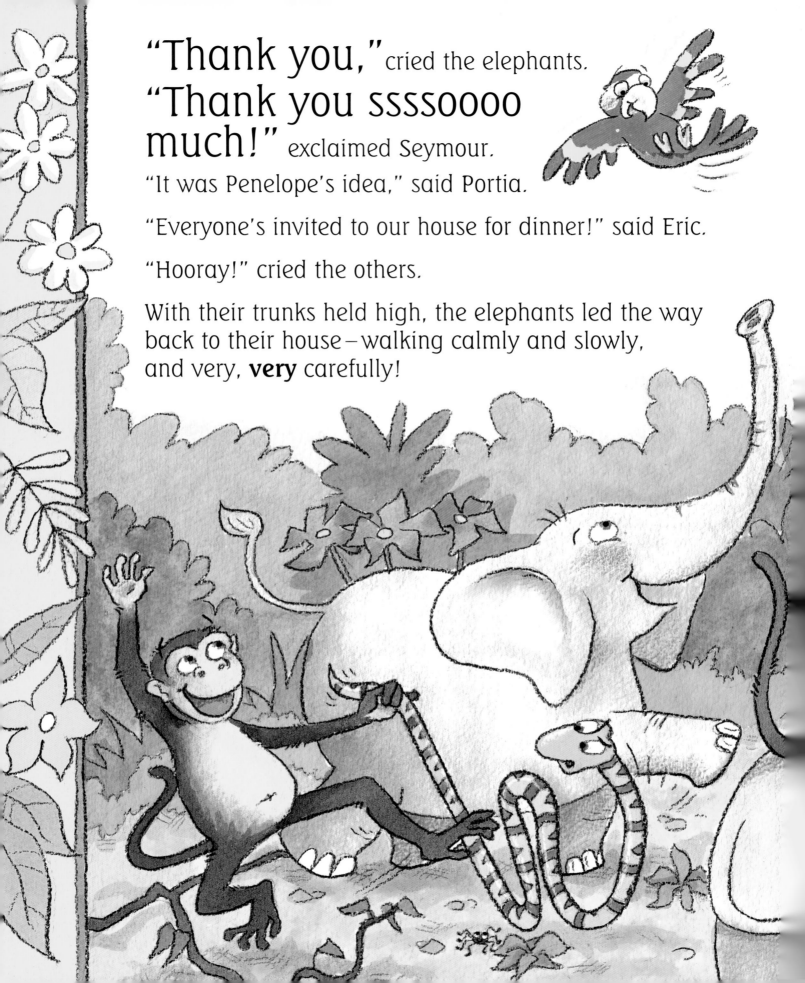

"Thank you," cried the elephants.
"Thank you sssssoooo much!" exclaimed Seymour.

"It was Penelope's idea," said Portia.

"Everyone's invited to our house for dinner!" said Eric.

"Hooray!" cried the others.

With their trunks held high, the elephants led the way back to their house—walking calmly and slowly, and very, **very** carefully!

The End

gym giraffe

Written by Ronne Randall
Illustrated by Jacqueline East

Jeremy Giraffe loved going out with his dad to gather the juicy green leaves for their dinner.

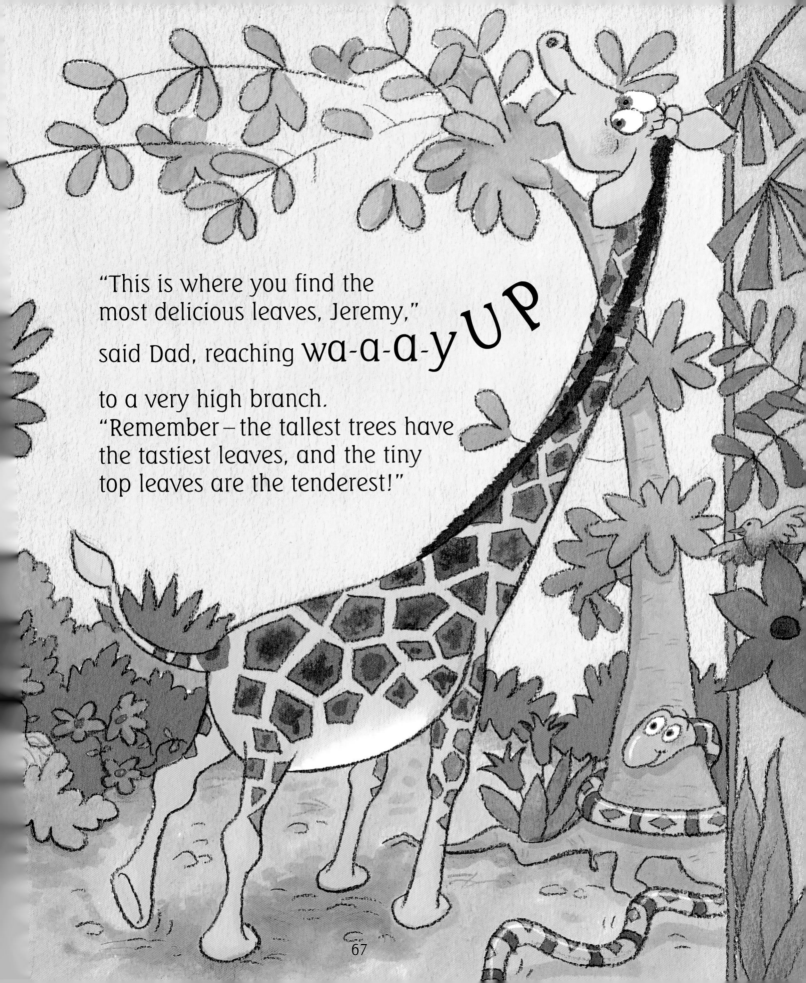

"This is where you find the
most delicious leaves, Jeremy,"
said Dad, reaching wa-a-a-y UP
to a very high branch.
"Remember – the tallest trees have
the tastiest leaves, and the tiny
top leaves are the tenderest!"

67

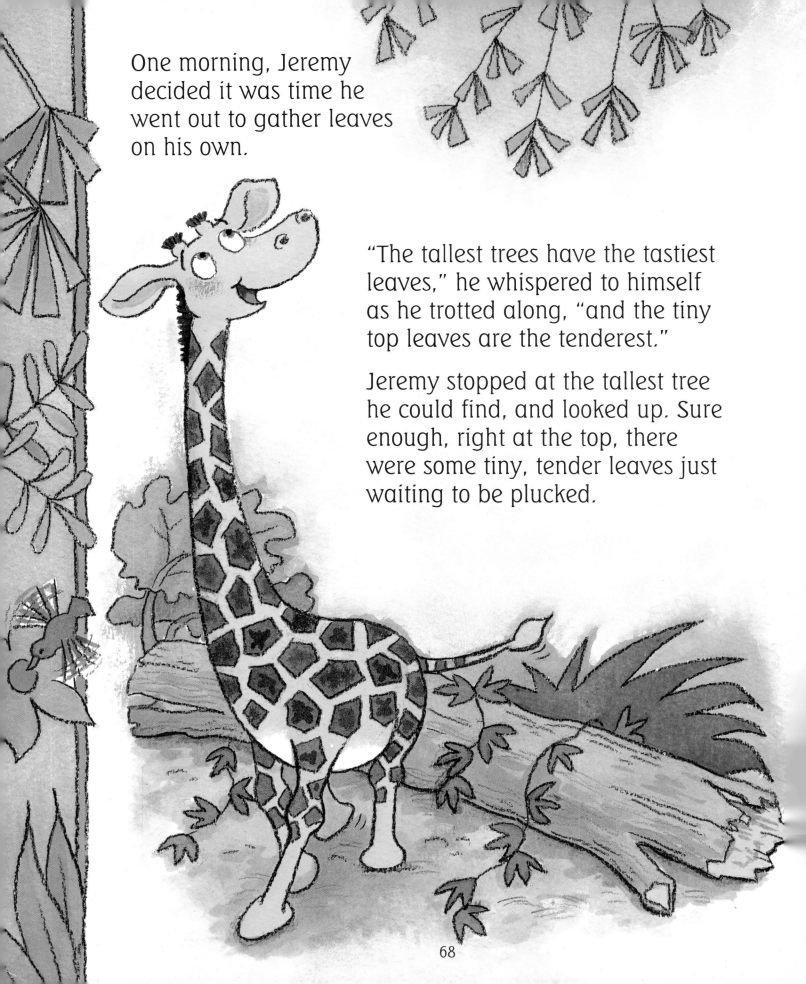

One morning, Jeremy decided it was time he went out to gather leaves on his own.

"The tallest trees have the tastiest leaves," he whispered to himself as he trotted along, "and the tiny top leaves are the tenderest."

Jeremy stopped at the tallest tree he could find, and looked up. Sure enough, right at the top, there were some tiny, tender leaves just waiting to be plucked.

Stre-e-e-e-etching

his neck just as he had seen his dad do, Jeremy reached as high as he could – it wasn't very high!

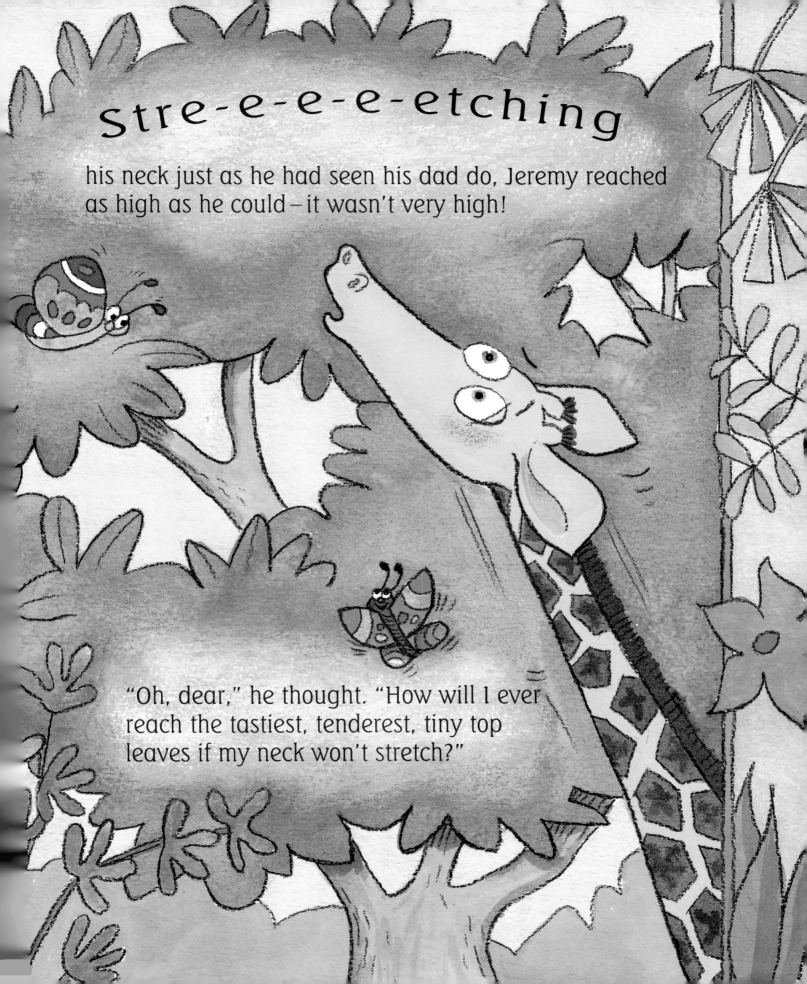

"Oh, dear," he thought. "How will I ever reach the tastiest, tenderest, tiny top leaves if my neck won't stretch?"

So Jeremy went back home with his neck hanging down in despair.

"Why, Jeremy, whatever is the matter?" asked his mum. When Jeremy told her, she gave his neck a nuzzle.

"You're still growing," she assured him. "Just eat your greens and get lots of sleep, and your neck will soon be long enough to reach the tastiest, tiniest, tenderest leaves on the tallest tree tops in the jungle!"

Jeremy couldn't wait for his neck to grow. That afternoon, he rushed out to try again.

High above him, Portia Parrot saw Jeremy struggling to reach the tiny leaves at the top of the tree. "He needs some help," she thought, so she swooped down and plucked a few of the tenderest leaves for him.

When Portia gave Jeremy the leaves, his spots went pale with shame and embarrassment.

"I should be able to get those myself," he wailed. "Why won't my neck stretch?"

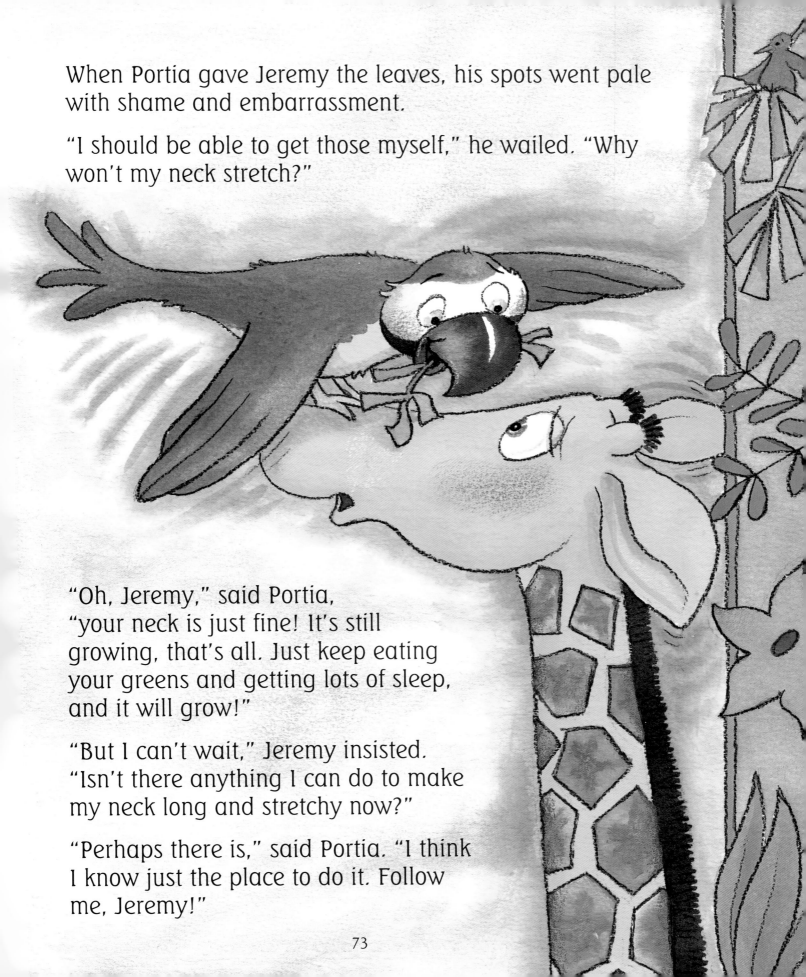

"Oh, Jeremy," said Portia, "your neck is just fine! It's still growing, that's all. Just keep eating your greens and getting lots of sleep, and it will grow!"

"But I can't wait," Jeremy insisted. "Isn't there anything I can do to make my neck long and stretchy now?"

"Perhaps there is," said Portia. "I think I know just the place to do it. Follow me, Jeremy!"

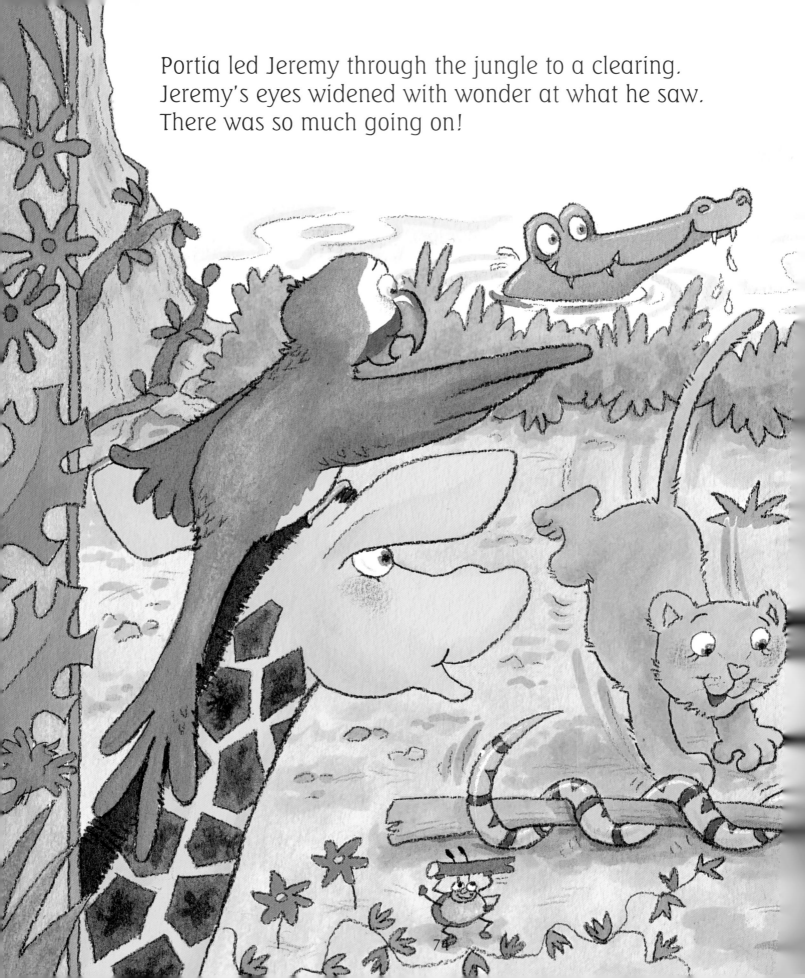

Portia led Jeremy through the jungle to a clearing.
Jeremy's eyes widened with wonder at what he saw.
There was so much going on!

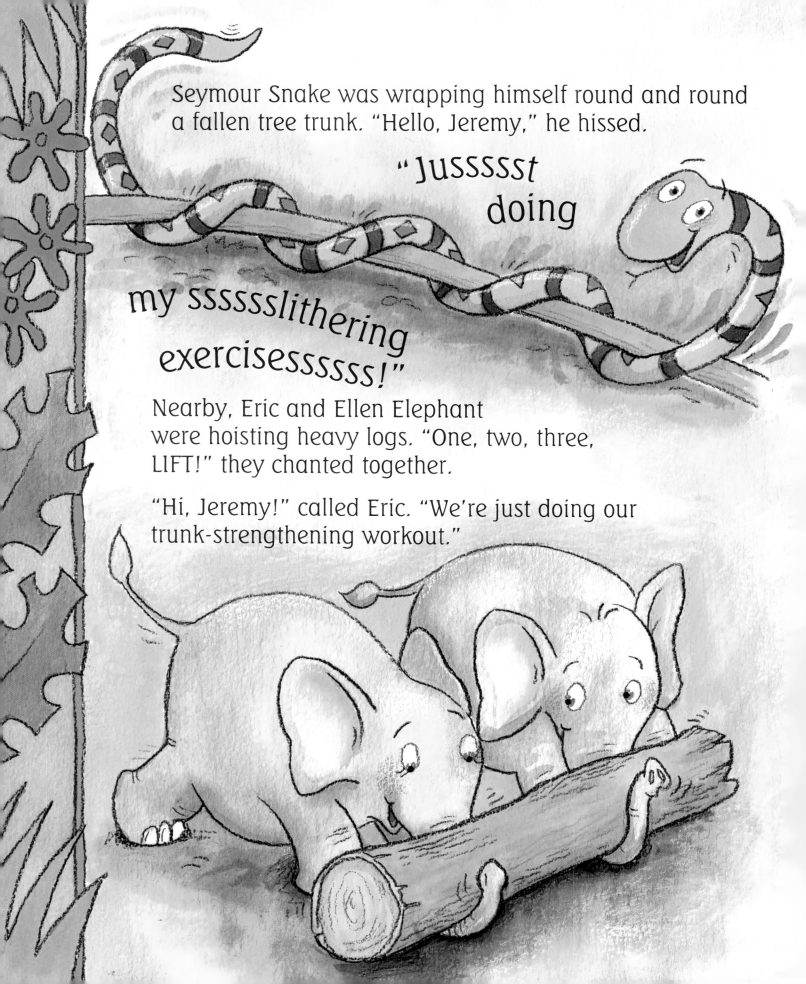

Seymour Snake was wrapping himself round and round a fallen tree trunk. "Hello, Jeremy," he hissed.

"Jussssst doing

my ssssssslithering exercisessssss!"

Nearby, Eric and Ellen Elephant were hoisting heavy logs. "One, two, three, LIFT!" they chanted together.

"Hi, Jeremy!" called Eric. "We're just doing our trunk-strengthening workout."

Near the riverbank, Grandpa Gorilla was holding out thick branches for Claudia Crocodile to break in half.

"Just limbering up my jaw muscles," Claudia snapped.

Leonard Lion was taking his own cubs, Louis and Lisa, through their pouncing paces. "Welcome to the Jungle Gym, Jeremy!" he called.

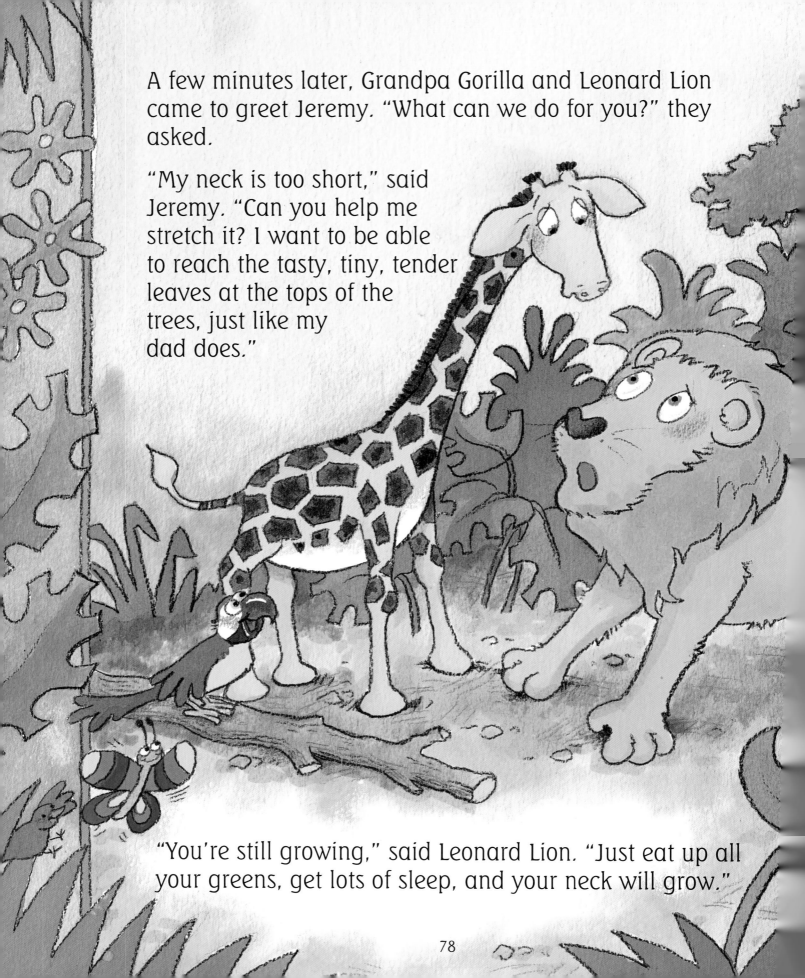

A few minutes later, Grandpa Gorilla and Leonard Lion came to greet Jeremy. "What can we do for you?" they asked.

"My neck is too short," said Jeremy. "Can you help me stretch it? I want to be able to reach the tasty, tiny, tender leaves at the tops of the trees, just like my dad does."

"You're still growing," said Leonard Lion. "Just eat up all your greens, get lots of sleep, and your neck will grow."

Jeremy's face fell. But he brightened up when Grandpa Gorilla said, "In the meantime, we can give you a special programme of neck-stretching exercises to help things along. Come with us!"

Grandpa got Jeremy started right away.
"S-t-r-e-t-c-h to the left!
S-t-r-e-t-c-h to the right!"
Grandpa Gorilla shouted.

"Left!

Left!

Right!

Right!"

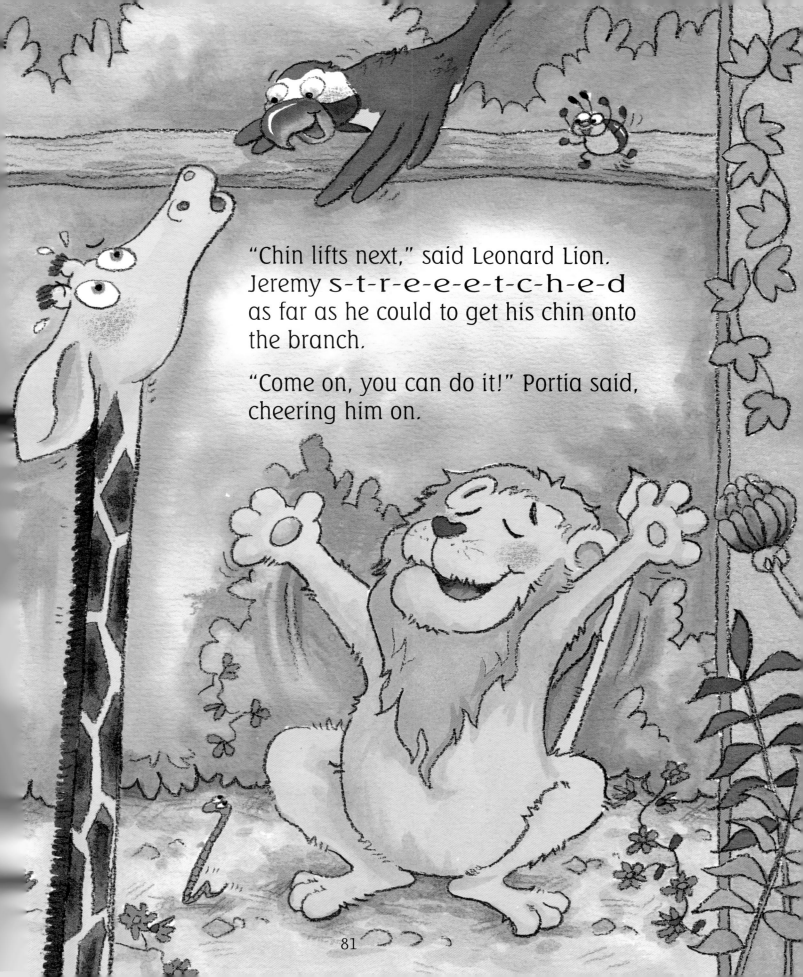

"Chin lifts next," said Leonard Lion.
Jeremy s-t-r-e-e-e-t-c-h-e-d
as far as he could to get his chin onto
the branch.

"Come on, you can do it!" Portia said,
cheering him on.

"I think Seymour can help with the next one," said Grandpa Gorilla. "Jeremy, you get down on the ground, and Seymour – start slithering!"

"Aaaakkk!"

gasped Jeremy, as Seymour wrapped himself round his neck.

"Er… not quite so tight, Seymour," said Grandpa.

"Aaaaahh!" sighed Jeremy. "That's better!" Seymour slithered along, pu-u-u-l-l-ing Jeremy's neck muscles as he went.

83

All the exercise made Jeremy really hungry. At supper that evening, he had three BIG helpings of greens.

He was tired, too, so he went to bed early and slept soundly all night.

Jeremy couldn't wait to get back to the Jungle Gym and do some more neck-stretching exercises. He went back the next day, the day after that, and the day after that.

"You're making excellent progress, Jeremy," Leonard Lion told him.

Every evening after his workout, Jeremy ate a good supper.

"Exercising makes me soooo hungry..." he told his mum and dad...

"and so000

tired," he yawned, as he settled down to sleep.

A few days later, Jeremy and his dad went out leaf-gathering together. Suddenly, Jeremy spotted a brand-new bunch of succulent, sweet-looking leaves right at the top of a tall tree.

"I'm going to get those, Dad," he said.

"But Jeremy," said Dad, "they're so high up!"

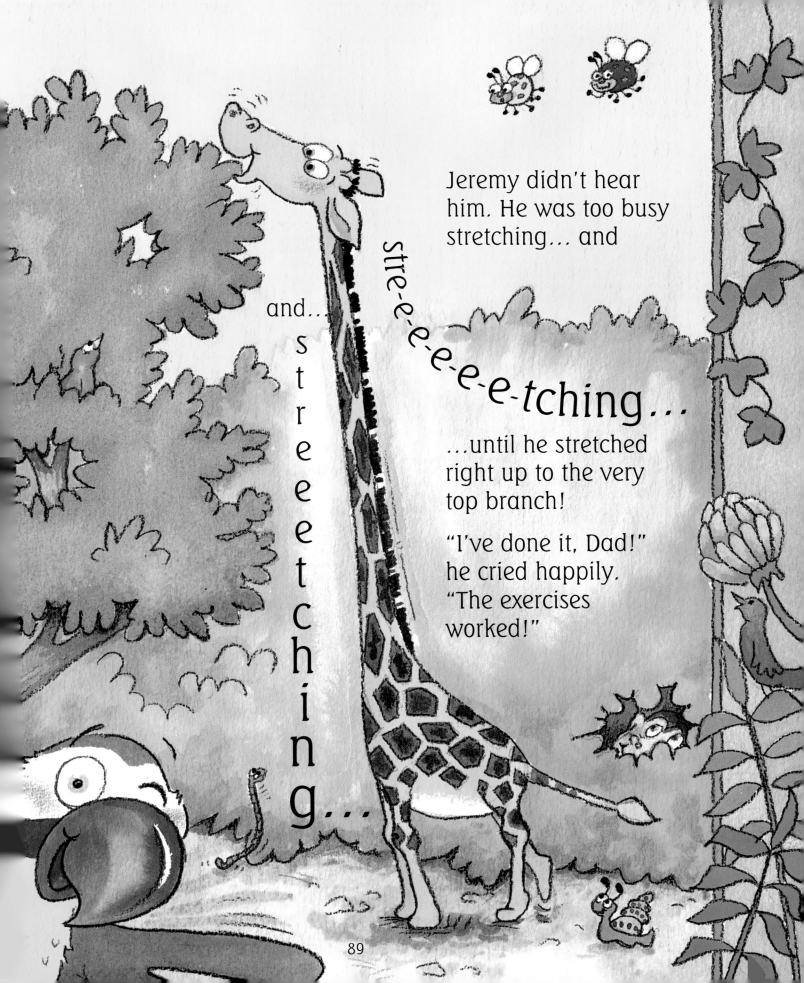

Jeremy didn't hear him. He was too busy stretching... and

stre-e-e-e-tching...

and... streeetching...

...until he stretched right up to the very top branch!

"I've done it, Dad!" he cried happily. "The exercises worked!"

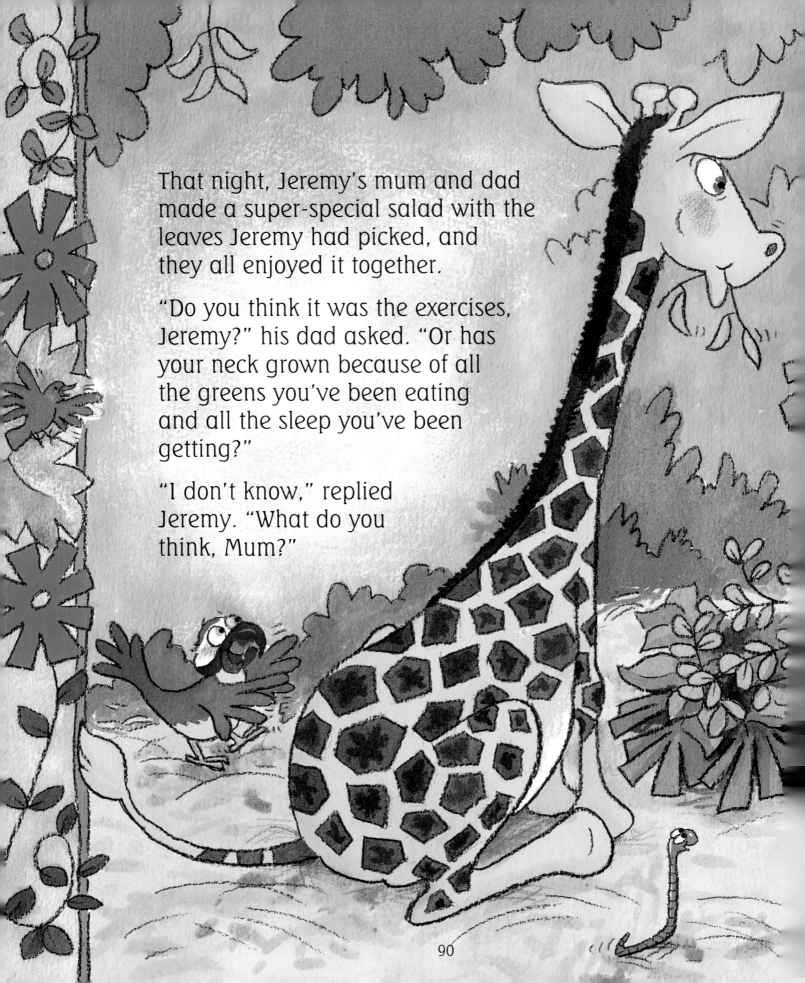

That night, Jeremy's mum and dad
made a super-special salad with the
leaves Jeremy had picked, and
they all enjoyed it together.

"Do you think it was the exercises,
Jeremy?" his dad asked. "Or has
your neck grown because of all
the greens you've been eating
and all the sleep you've been
getting?"

"I don't know," replied
Jeremy. "What do you
think, Mum?"

"I think it doesn't matter at all," replied Mum. "What matters is that you have a fine, strong, lo-o-o-o-ng neck that any giraffe would be proud of!"

"And I am!" said Jeremy, taking another mouthful of tasty, tender leaves. He chewed the leaves extra thoroughly – because he knew they had a very long way to go!

The End

tiger tales

Written by Ronne Randall
Illustrated by Jacqueline East

Louis and Lisa Lion were just learning to pounce, and their dad had told them to practise as much as they could. So they were prowling through the jungle, looking for prey to pounce upon.

"There's something orange and blue and fluttery," whispered Lisa. "Here I go…"

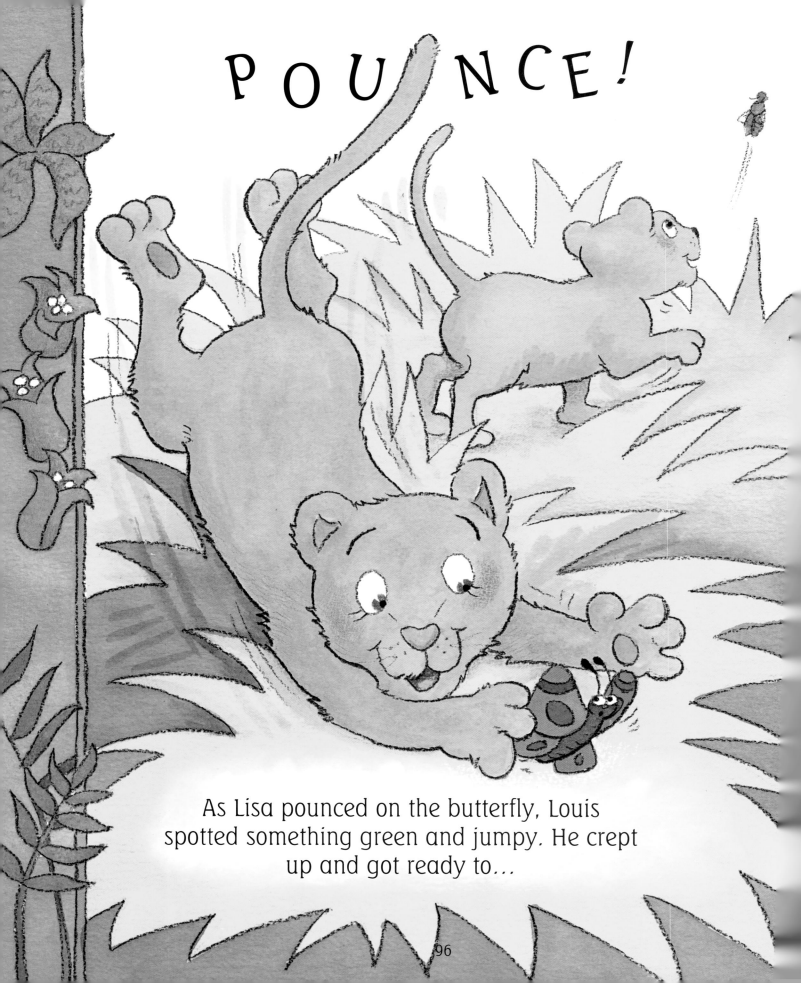

POUNCE!

As Lisa pounced on the butterfly, Louis spotted something green and jumpy. He crept up and got ready to...

POUNCE!

Just then, Lisa caught a glimpse of black and yellow fuzz. "Perfect for pouncing," she thought. "Ready, steady…"

POUNCE!

"OUCH!"

cried Lisa, rubbing
her nose with her paw.

"Maybe a bumble-bee isn't such a good pouncing target! In fact, I think I've had enough pouncing practice for one day."

"Me too," said Louis. "Let's find something else to do."

But as the two little cubs bounded through the jungle, Louis suddenly saw a flash of orange and black in some bushes.

"A stripey snake!" he whispered. "It's too good to pass up!" So he crouched down and waited and waited for just the right moment, and then he...

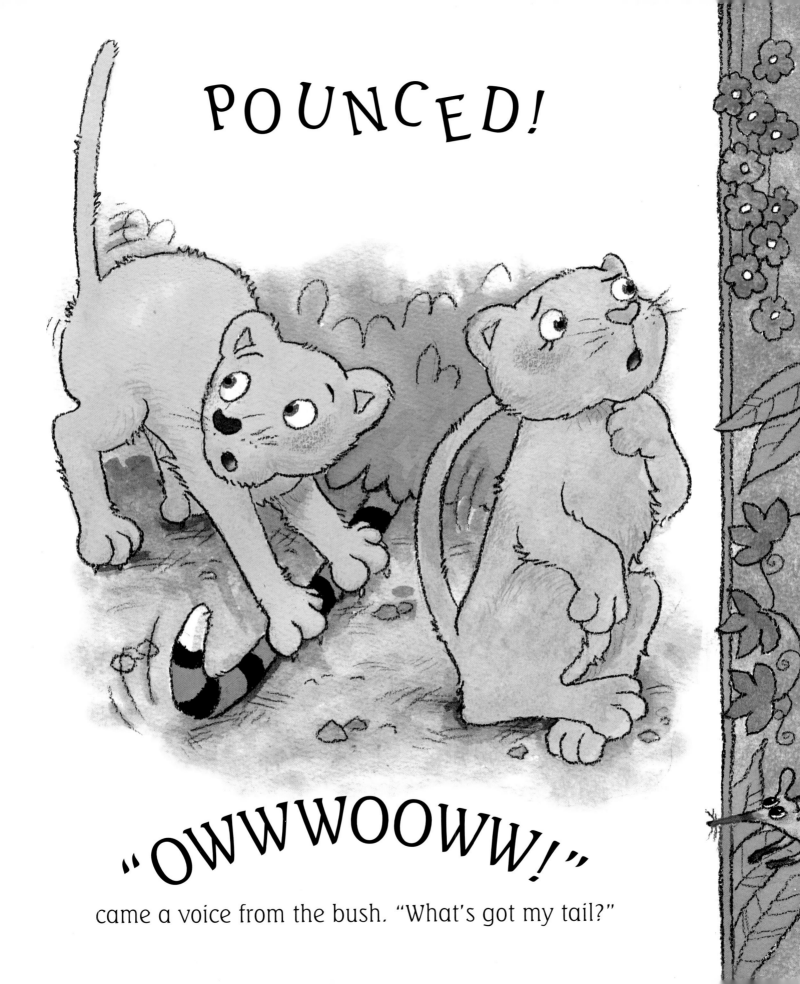

POUNCED!

"OWWWOOWW!"

came a voice from the bush. "What's got my tail?"

The 'snake' turned out to be attached to a stripey little cub, just the same size as Louis and Lisa!

"Who are you?" they asked.

"I'm Timmy Tiger," said the little cub. "My mum and dad and I have just moved here from The Other Side of the Jungle. Who are you?"

"We're Louis and Lisa Lion," said Lisa. "Would you like to see what this side of the jungle looks like?"

Timmy said he would love to.

"That's our river," said Louis proudly. "It's really muddy, and fun to paddle in."

"It's very nice," said Timmy, "but it's kind of small. On The Other Side of the Jungle, there's a river that's as wide as fifty tall palm trees laid end to end!"

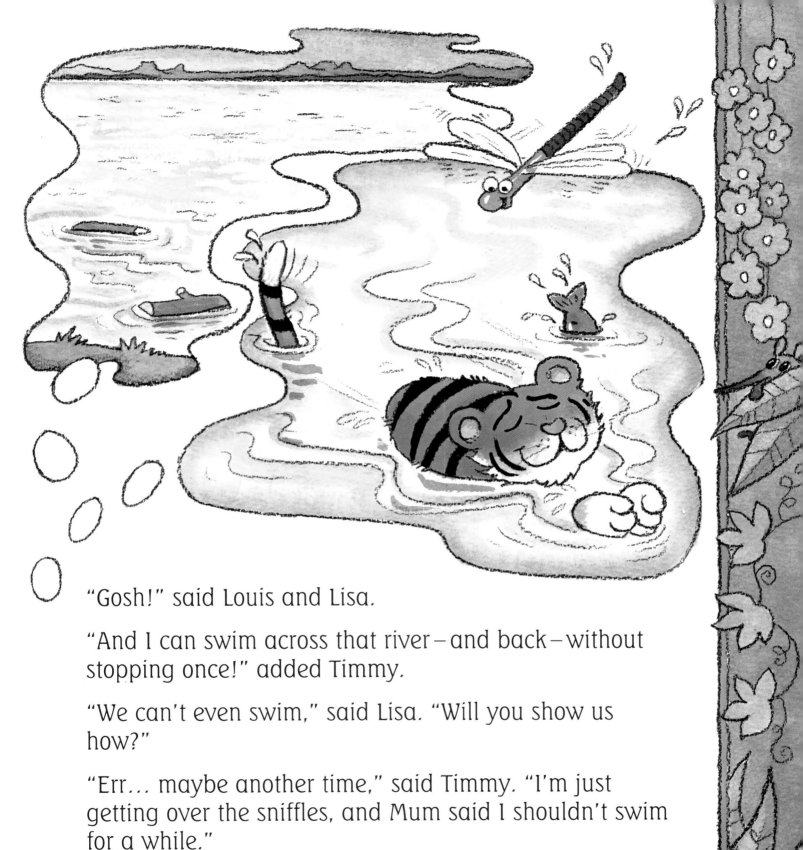

"Gosh!" said Louis and Lisa.

"And I can swim across that river – and back – without stopping once!" added Timmy.

"We can't even swim," said Lisa. "Will you show us how?"

"Err… maybe another time," said Timmy. "I'm just getting over the sniffles, and Mum said I shouldn't swim for a while."

A little farther along, Louis and Lisa saw Howard Hippo wallowing merrily in the mud.

"Hi, Howard!" they called. "This is our new friend, Timmy Tiger!"

Howard opened his mouth in a happy hippo grin. "Nice to meet you!" he bellowed.

"Nice to meet you, too," said Timmy, keeping his distance.

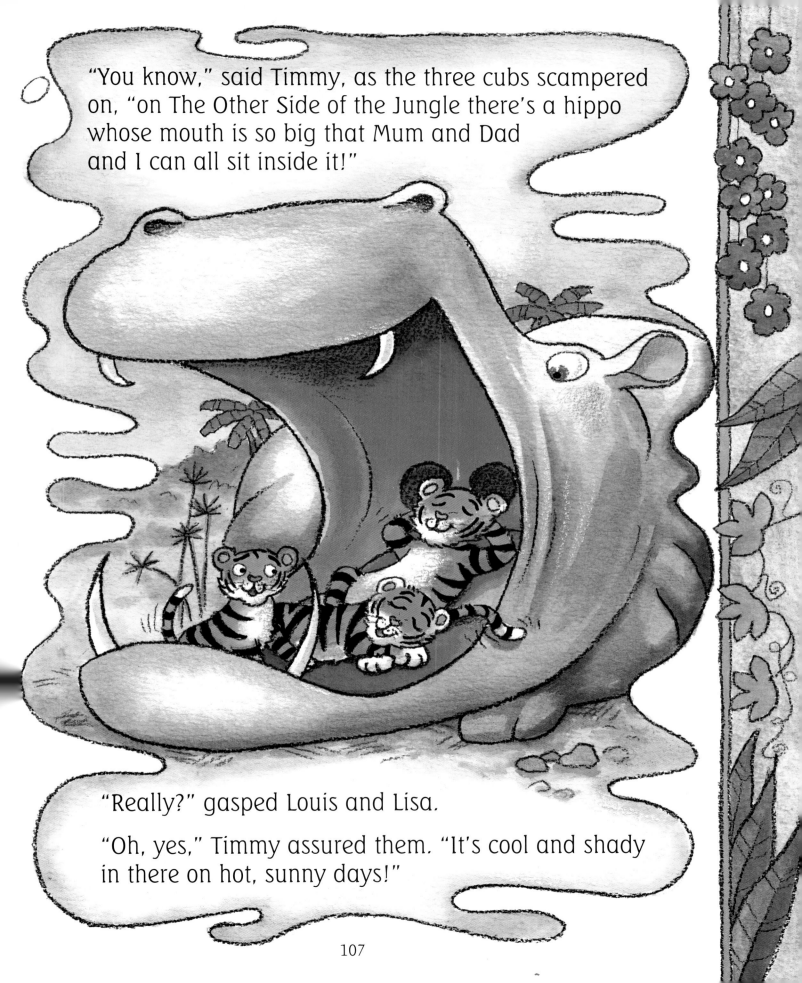

"You know," said Timmy, as the three cubs scampered on, "on The Other Side of the Jungle there's a hippo whose mouth is so big that Mum and Dad and I can all sit inside it!"

"Really?" gasped Louis and Lisa.

"Oh, yes," Timmy assured them. "It's cool and shady in there on hot, sunny days!"

Before Louis and Lisa had a chance to think about that, something dropped down from a branch, right in front of them. Timmy jumped back, but Louis and Lisa smiled and said, "Hi, Seymour! Meet our new friend, Timmy Tiger."

"Greetingsssss," hissed

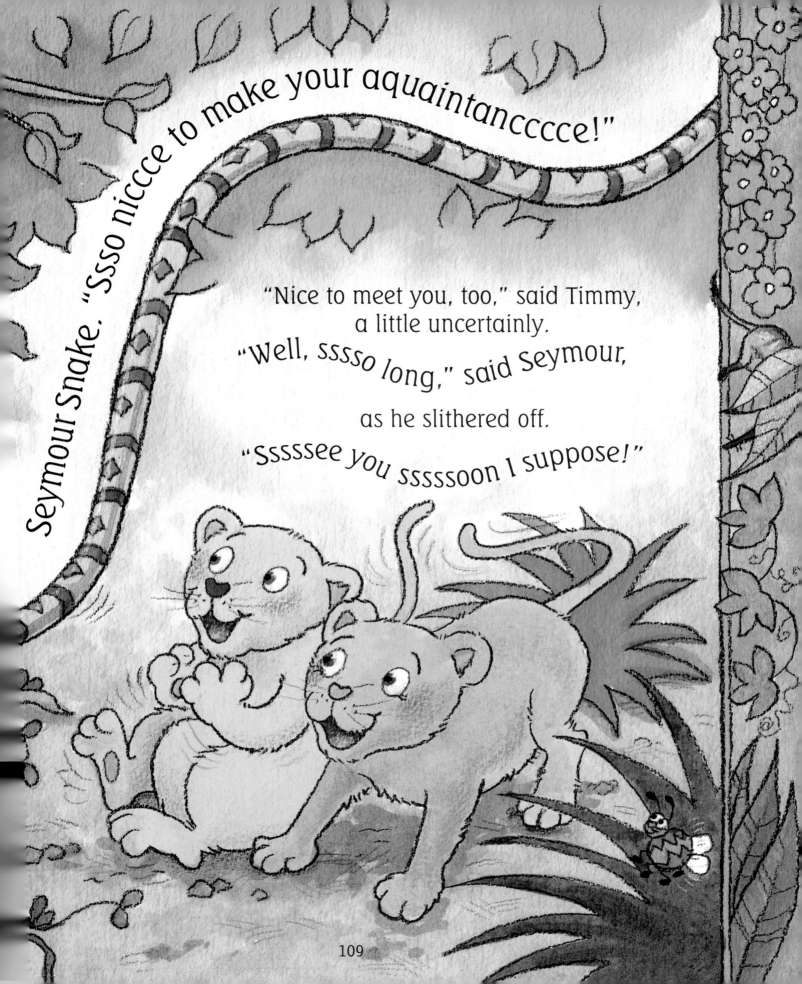

Seymour Snake. "Ssso niccce to make your aquaintancccce!"

"Nice to meet you, too," said Timmy, a little uncertainly.

"Well, sssso long," said Seymour, as he slithered off.

"Ssssssee you sssssoon I suppose!"

As Seymour disappeared down the path, Timmy said, "On The Other Side of the Jungle, there are snakes as thick as tree trunks. In fact, when I was a baby, one of those snakes swallowed me whole!"

"Oh, no!" cried Louis and Lisa.

"Yes," Timmy went on, "but my dad saved me by hitting the snake on the head so that he would spit me out!"

"Really?" said Louis and Lisa, their eyes growing wider and wider.

"Yes," said Timmy. "My dad's really, really strong, and really, really big. He's twice as big as an elephant, and he can carry six gorillas on his back! And my mum can do amazing things. She can stand on her front paws and juggle coconuts with her hind legs, and… and…"

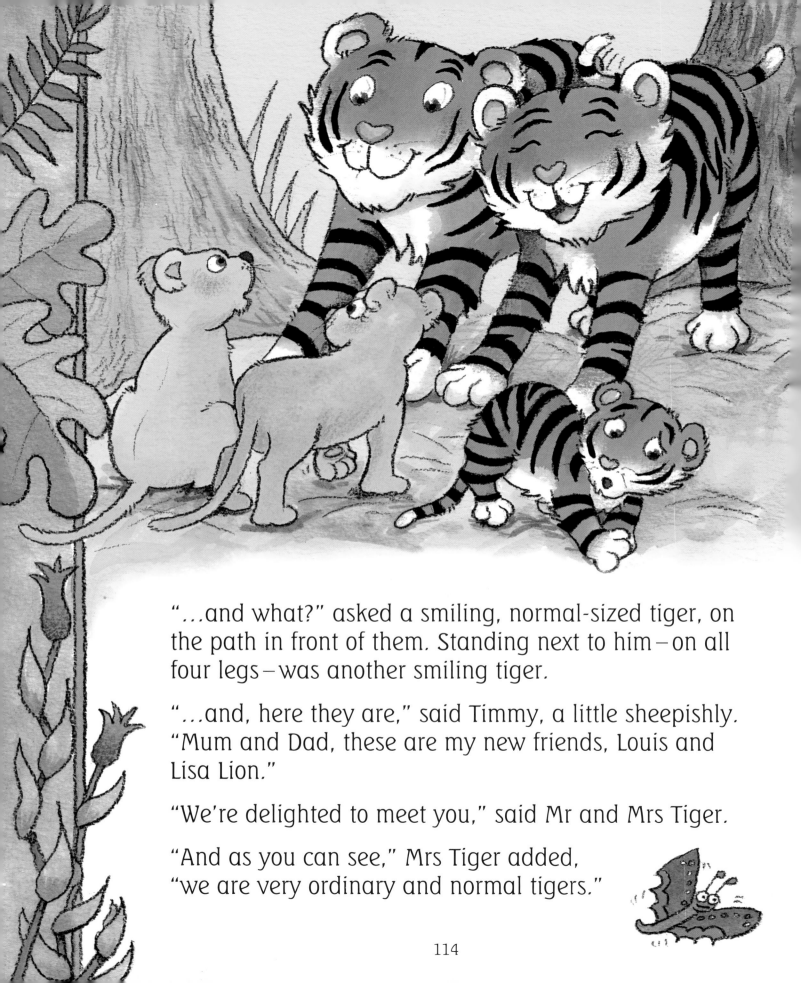

"…and what?" asked a smiling, normal-sized tiger, on the path in front of them. Standing next to him – on all four legs – was another smiling tiger.

"…and, here they are," said Timmy, a little sheepishly. "Mum and Dad, these are my new friends, Louis and Lisa Lion."

"We're delighted to meet you," said Mr and Mrs Tiger.

"And as you can see," Mrs Tiger added, "we are very ordinary and normal tigers."

"But what about all those amazing things Timmy told us?" asked Louis. "What about The Other Side of the Jungle?"

"The Other Side of the Jungle is just like this side," said Mr Tiger.

"You mean the river isn't as wide as fifty tall palm trees laid end to end?" asked Lisa.

"And there isn't a hippo whose mouth is big enough to sit in, or a snake who swallowed Timmy when he was a baby?"

"No, indeed!" laughed Mrs Tiger.

Timmy looked embarrassed. "Well, they were good stories," he said.

"Yes," said Mrs Tiger, "but they were just stories." She turned to Louis and Lisa. "Timmy didn't have any friends to play with on The Other Side of the Jungle, so he spent all his time making up fantastic stories and imagining amazing adventures."

"But now that he's got friends like you two to play with," said Mr Tiger, "perhaps he'll have some real adventures, just as exciting as the ones in his stories!"

116

"And there are still more friends to meet, Timmy," Lisa said. "Wait till we introduce you to Mickey and Maxine Monkey, and Chico Chimp!"

"You know, there are monkeys and chimps on The Other Side of the Jungle, too," said Timmy.

"Really?" said Louis and Lisa, glancing at one another.

"Yes," said Timmy, "but actually, I didn't know them. I can't wait to meet Mickey and Maxine and Chico!"

"Well, what are we waiting for?" said Louis, and the three bounded off together, ready for fun and excitement on *This Side* of the Jungle.

The End

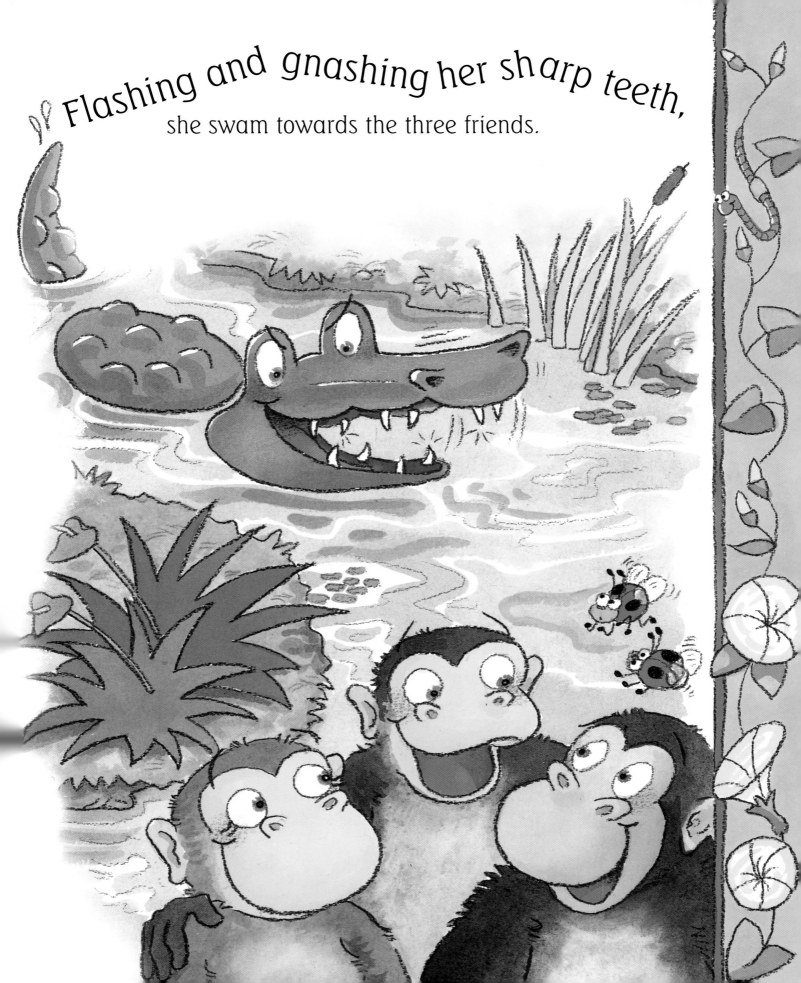

Flashing and gnashing her sharp teeth,
she swam towards the three friends.

Sure enough, the

SNAP! SNAP! SNAP!

of Claudia's big, strong jaws scared the little monkeys.

"RUN," cried Maxine, "before she snaps our tails off!"

They tumbled over each other in their rush to climb up to safety in a tall tree.

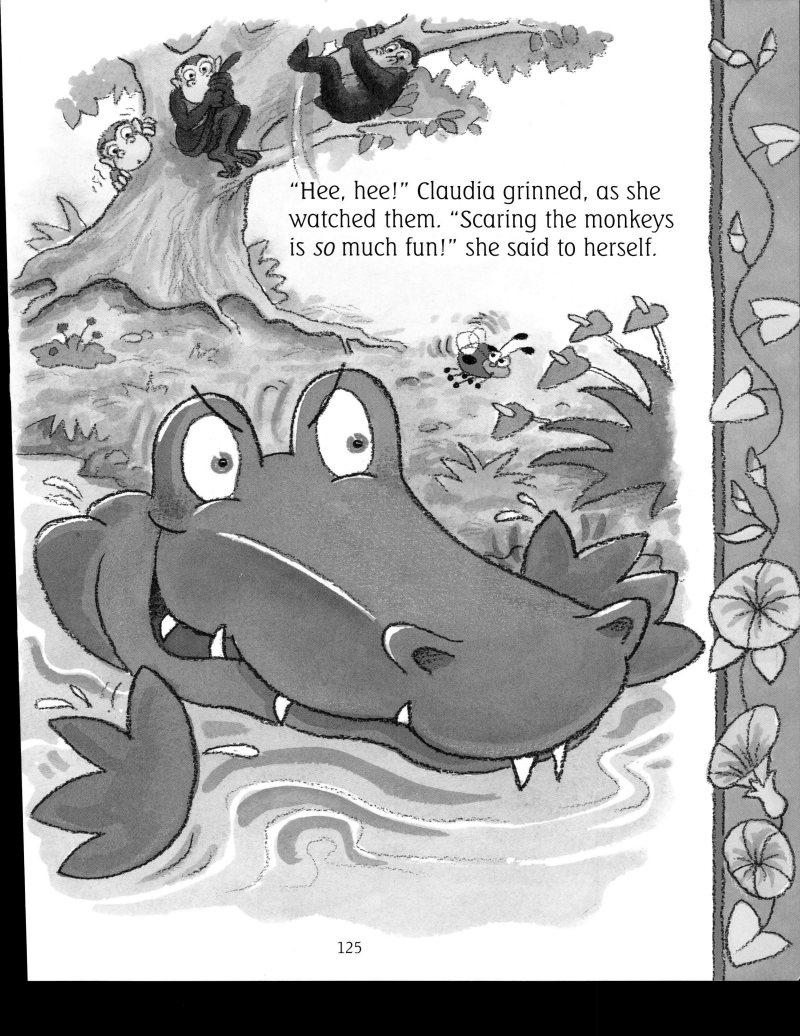

"Hee, hee!" Claudia grinned, as she watched them. "Scaring the monkeys is *so* much fun!" she said to herself.

125

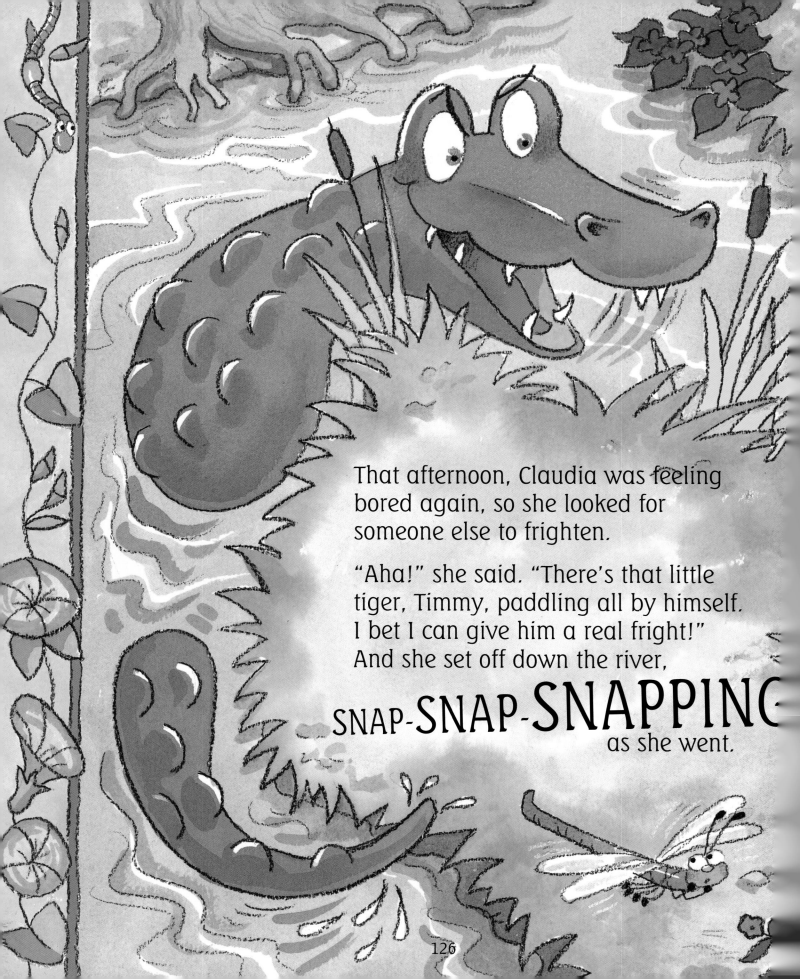

That afternoon, Claudia was feeling bored again, so she looked for someone else to frighten.

"Aha!" she said. "There's that little tiger, Timmy, paddling all by himself. I bet I can give him a real fright!" And she set off down the river,

SNAP-SNAP-SNAPPING as she went.

Timmy was lost in a daydream, so he didn't hear Claudia, until she was right behind him! SNAP! SNAP! went her great big jaws.

GNASH! GNASH! GNASH!

went her sharp, pointy teeth.

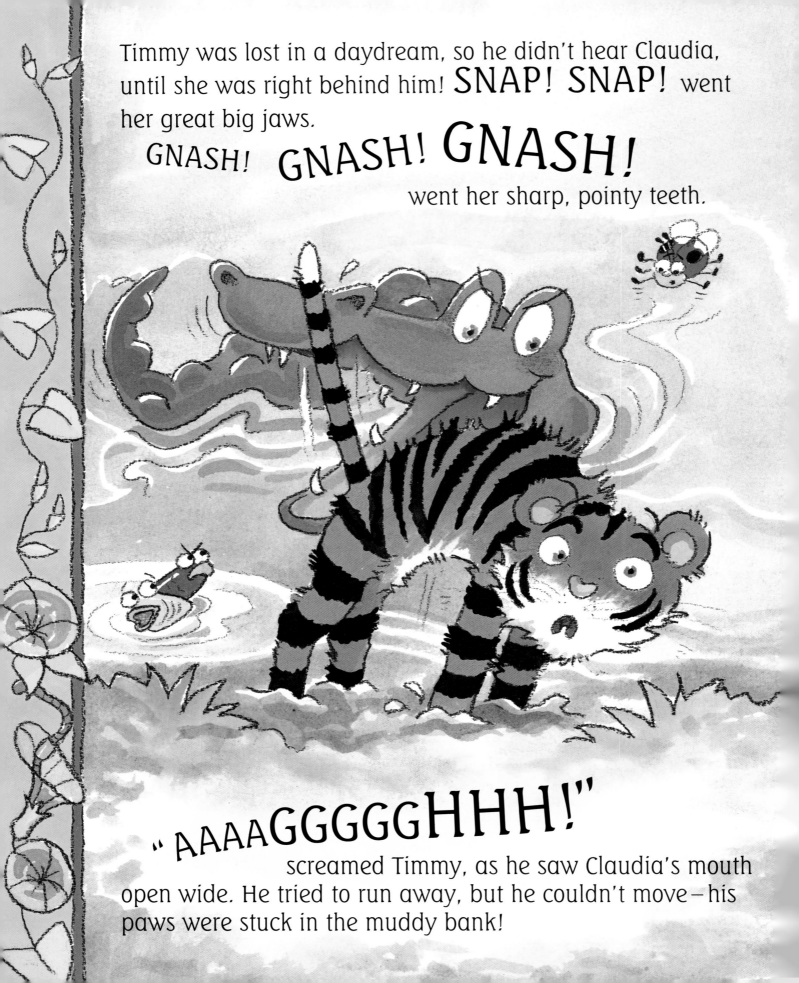

"AAAAGGGGGHHH!"

screamed Timmy, as he saw Claudia's mouth open wide. He tried to run away, but he couldn't move – his paws were stuck in the muddy bank!

Claudia came closer and closer – until her snout was right next to Timmy's ear.

He was trembling with terror.

"You're supposed to run away!" Claudia whispered.

"I c-c-can't," stammered Timmy. "I'm stuck!"

"Oh," said Claudia, disappointed. "It's no fun if you don't run away."

"Y-You m-mean you're n-not going to eat me?" gulped Timmy.

"EAT YOU?" roared Claudia. "Yuck! You're covered in fur! I prefer fish."

"Really?" said Timmy, his eyes wide with surprise. "Then why are you always snapping your jaws and gnashing your teeth and frightening everyone?"

"Because that's what crocodiles do!" said Claudia. "We're supposed to be scary. Er… you won't tell anyone that I didn't eat you, will you?" she asked, as she helped Timmy out of the mud.

"Don't worry," laughed Timmy, "I won't tell anyone."

"And thanks for getting me un-stuck," Timmy continued. "I never knew you could be nice. I like you!"

Claudia's green face blushed bright red! "No one's ever said that to me before," she said.

"Well, I think everyone would like you," said Timmy, "if you could just be friendly, instead of scary."

"Oh, I don't think I can do that," said Claudia, turning to leave. "I mean, my jaws simply have to SNAP and my teeth just must GNASH! I can't help it."

"Wait!" said Timmy. "I think I know how you can be friendly and helpful and snap and gnash at the same time! Come with me."

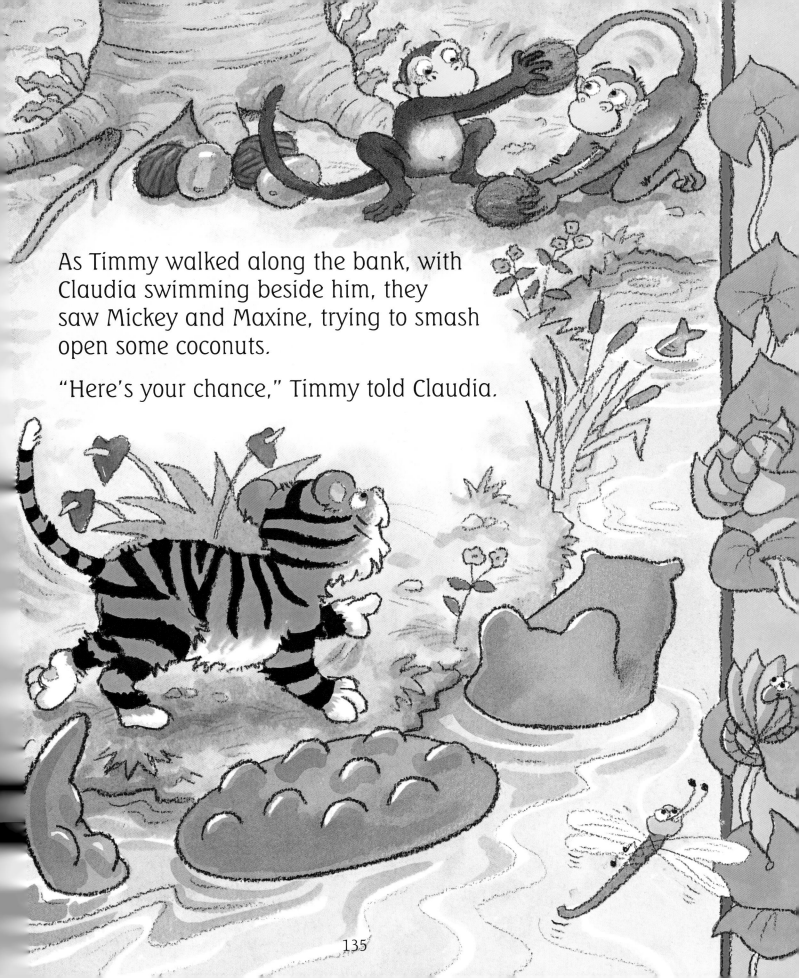

As Timmy walked along the bank, with Claudia swimming beside him, they saw Mickey and Maxine, trying to smash open some coconuts.

"Here's your chance," Timmy told Claudia.

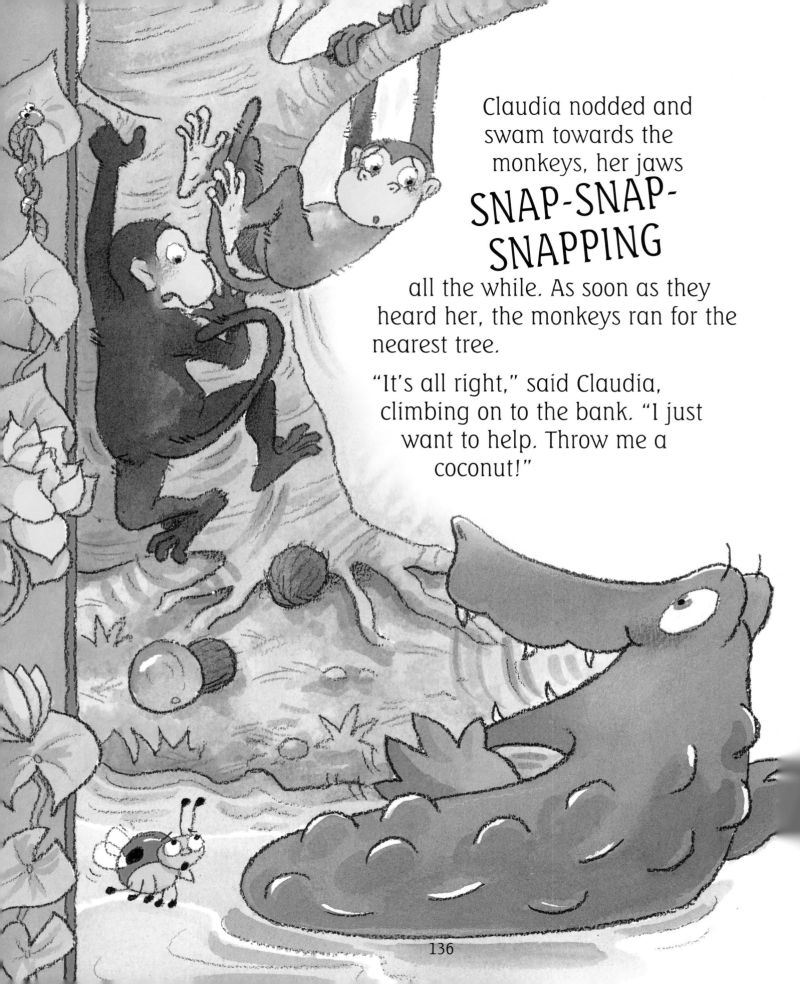

Claudia nodded and swam towards the monkeys, her jaws

SNAP-SNAP-SNAPPING

all the while. As soon as they heard her, the monkeys ran for the nearest tree.

"It's all right," said Claudia, climbing on to the bank. "I just want to help. Throw me a coconut!"

The monkeys were uncertain, but Mickey tossed his coconut at Claudia's gaping jaw.

SNAP! SNAP! SNAP!

Quick as a flash, the coconut was open. "Gosh, Claudia, thanks!" said an amazed Mickey.

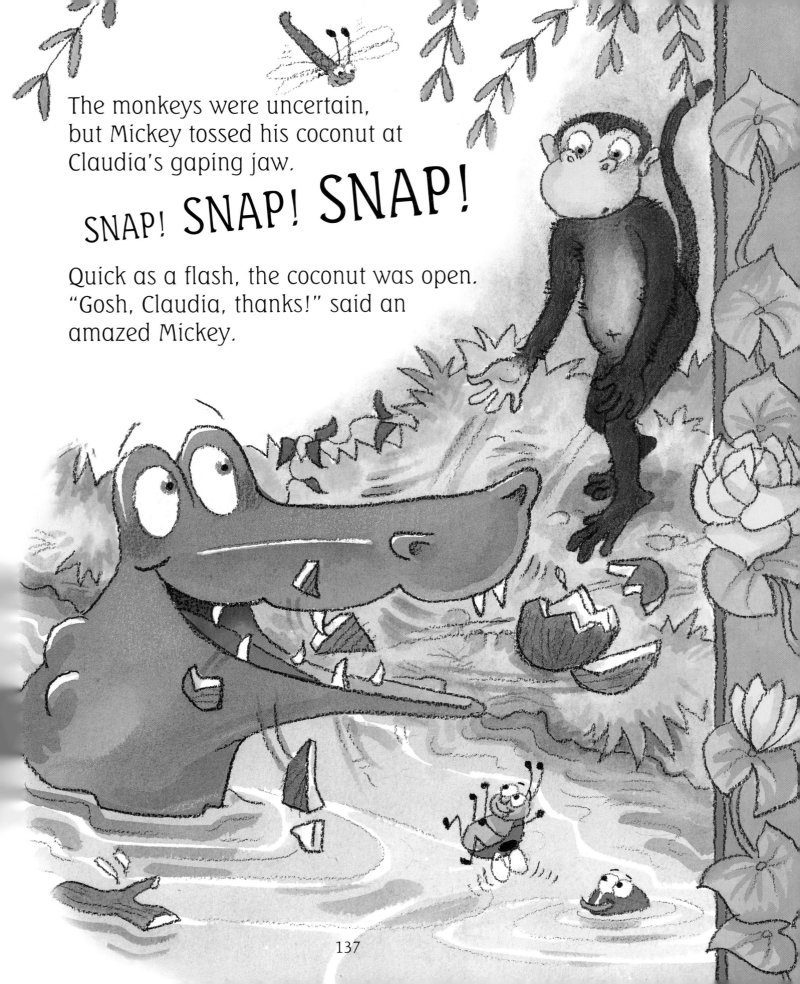

Claudia opened Maxine's coconut, too. Soon, everyone was sharing the cool, refreshing milk and chomping on chewy chunks of coconut.

Claudia had never shared anything with anyone else before. She was surprised to discover that she liked it!

"Hey, guys, look what I found!" called Chico Chimp, running towards his friends. He was carrying a big watermelon.

Suddenly, Chico spotted Claudia, whose jaw was open, ready to

SNAP!

"Uh-oh!" he gulped, turning to run.

"Don't worry, Chico," said Maxine. "Throw Claudia the watermelon!"

Chico did and watched in amazement, as Claudia SNAP- SNAP- SNAPPED! the watermelon into neat slices for everyone.

"Thanks, Claudia!" they all chorused.
Chico gave Claudia the biggest slice.

Claudia and her new friends were having a wild watermelon-seed-spitting contest, when they saw Emma, Eric and Ellen Elephant, trundling down to the river. They were carrying bundles of thick branches in their trunks.

"We're going to make a raft!" said Emma.

"Yes," said Eric. "We just have to trim these branches down to the right size... OH, NO! It's Claudia!"

Claudia was coming towards them, jaws SNAP-SNAP-SNAPPING!

As the elephants galloped away, Claudia went for the branches they had dropped.

SNAP! SNAP! GNASH! GNASH! went Claudia's strong jaws and sharp teeth.

Claudia trimmed the branches to just the right size for raft-making.

"Wow! Thanks, Claudia!" said Emma, as the elephants came back. "That was really helpful!"

Claudia smiled a big crocodile grin. Being friendly and helpful was turning out to be much nicer than she'd expected.

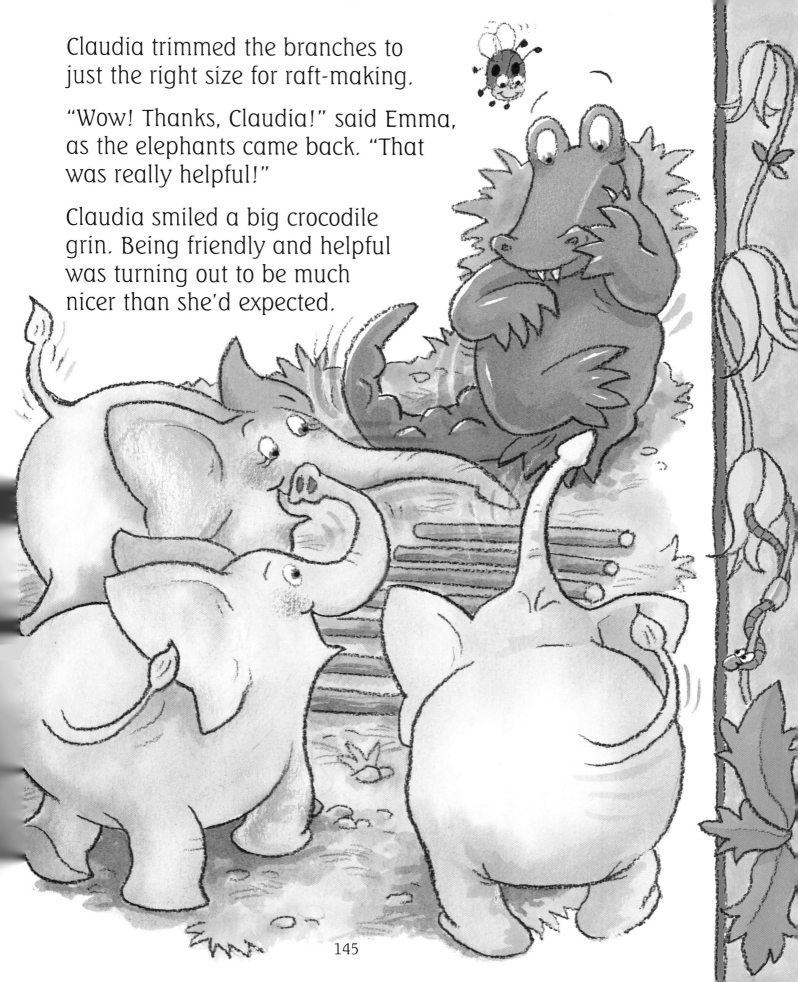

"Here we go!" shouted the elephants, when their raft was ready. The friends on the riverbank looked at them. Suddenly they had an idea…

"That looks like *so* much fun!" said Chico. "Can you help us make a raft, too, Claudia?"

"I can do better than that," said Claudia. "Hop on my back!"

Penelope Parrot and her mum, Portia, were having a wonderful afternoon, watching the Fancy Flying Display Team. Penelope could hardly believe her eyes, as she saw the birds swoop and speed through the sky, doing their amazing tricks and wonderful stunts.

That night, Penelope dreamt about doing magnificent stunts with the other birds...

...and, in the morning, she decided she would try to make her dream come true!

"I'm going to practise my flying, Mum," she said. "I want to be better than anybody!"

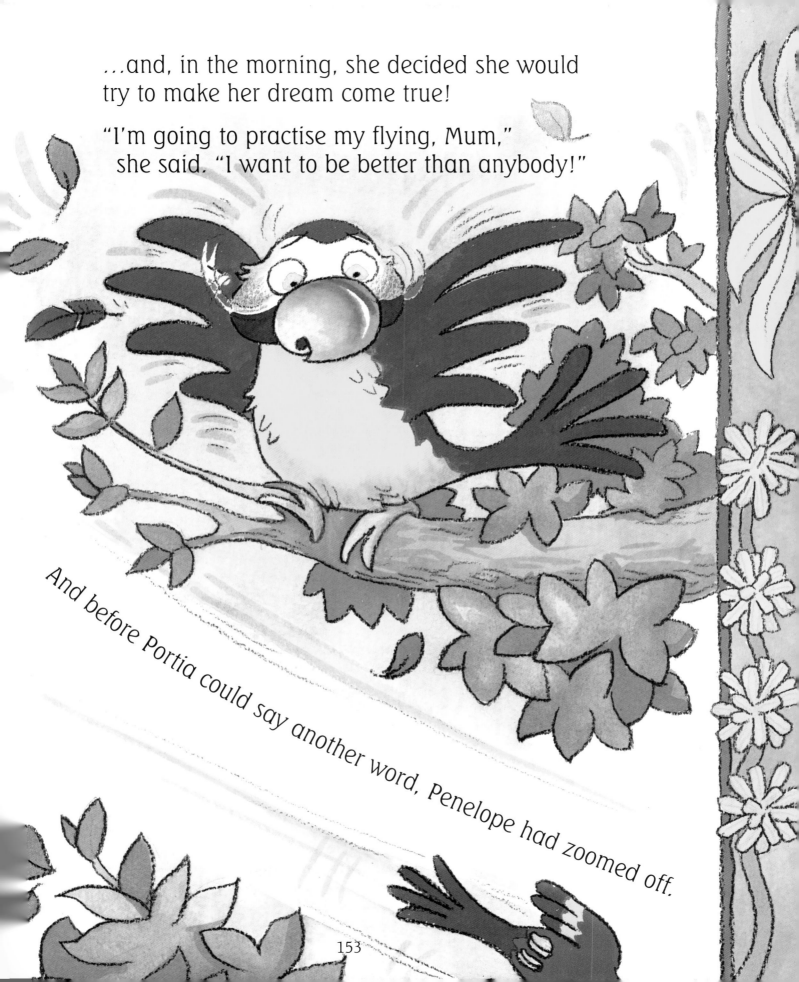

And before Portia could say another word, Penelope had zoomed off.

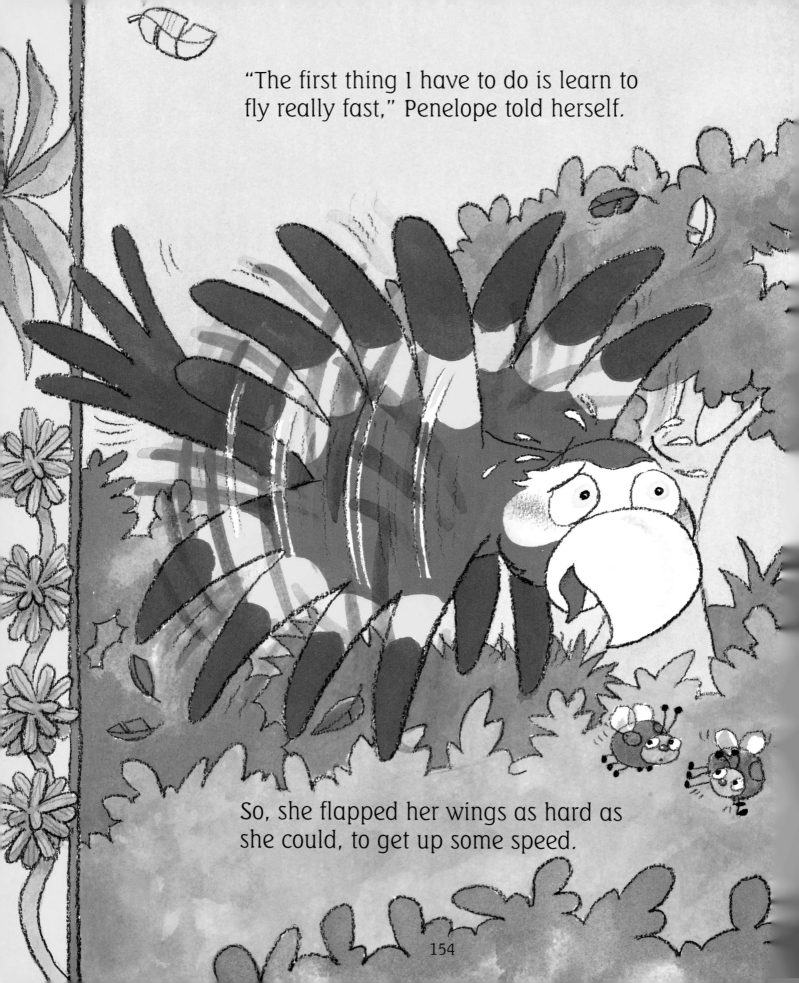

"The first thing I have to do is learn to
fly really fast," Penelope told herself.

So, she flapped her wings as hard as
she could, to get up some speed.

But Penelope had only learned to fly a short time ago—so she didn't really know how fast or how far she could go before her wings got tired. Soon, she was huffing and puffing and panting and her poor wings were flopping instead of flapping!

"Oh, nooooo!"

she cried, as she felt herself falling

down, down, down,

until...

...SPLASH!

She landed right in front of Howard Hippo, who had been enjoying a nice morning's wallow in the river.

"Gracious, Penelope," said Howard, trying to shake the water out of his eyes and ears. "You really should be more careful!"

"Sorry, Howard," said Penelope. "I didn't plan that dive. I was just seeing how fast I could fly and my wings got tired. I want to be a Fancy Flyer!"

"I think you need some expert training," said Howard.

"But I don't know any experts," said Penelope.

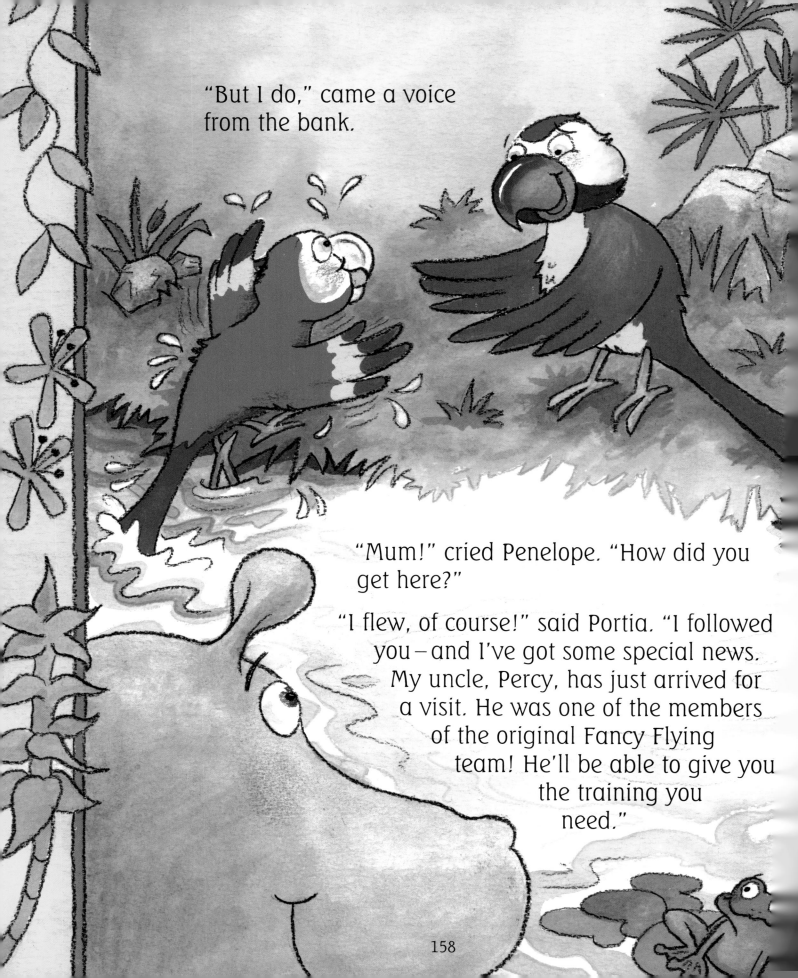

"But I do," came a voice from the bank.

"Mum!" cried Penelope. "How did you get here?"

"I flew, of course!" said Portia. "I followed you—and I've got some special news. My uncle, Percy, has just arrived for a visit. He was one of the members of the original Fancy Flying team! He'll be able to give you the training you need."

That afternoon, Uncle Percy
was delighted to meet Penelope —
and he was even more delighted when
he found out that she wanted to learn how
to be a Fancy Flyer.

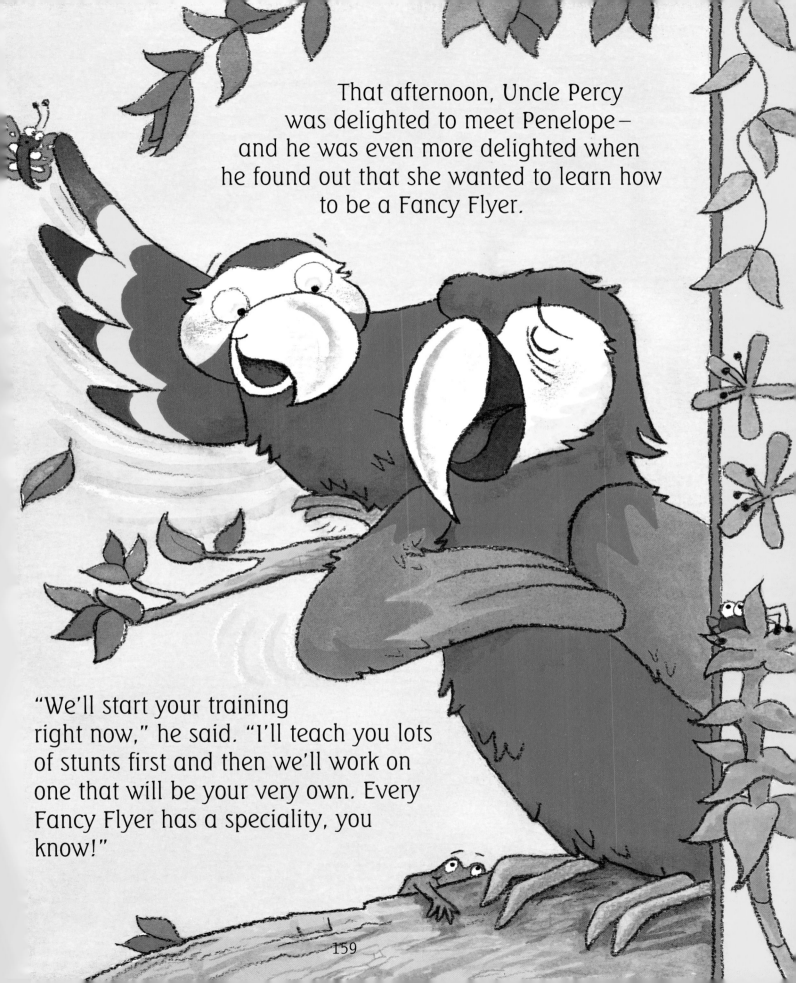

"We'll start your training
right now," he said. "I'll teach you lots
of stunts first and then we'll work on
one that will be your very own. Every
Fancy Flyer has a speciality, you
know!"

So, Uncle Percy and Penelope went to a quiet part of the jungle, to start her training programme.

"We'll begin with the Twisting Take Off," Uncle Percy said. "Just watch me and do what I do."

160

"Now, straighten up and fly forward!" Percy called.

But Penelope couldn't stop spinning and spinning!

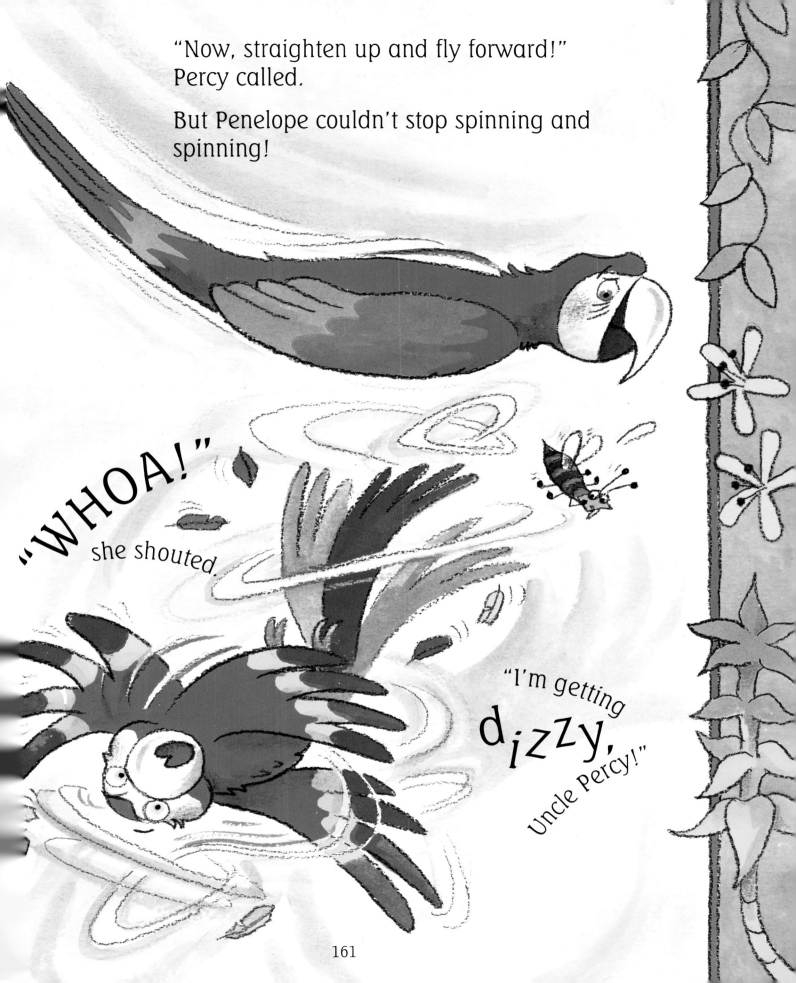

"WHOA!" she shouted.

"I'm getting dizzy, Uncle Percy!"

161

Luckily, Penelope grabbed a branch and managed to stop spinning at last.

Jeremy Giraffe, who was nibbling some leaves nearby, helped Penelope up as Uncle Percy flew back to join her.

"Never mind," said Uncle Percy. "You'll get the hang of it soon enough."

Just then, Penelope's friends, Mickey, Maxine and Chico, came swinging through the branches.

"Hi, Penelope!" they called. "Want to play Mango-Catch with us? You can be Parrot-in-the-Middle!"

"Great!" said Penelope, flying over to join them.

"Just one moment!" said Uncle Percy. "When a Fancy Flyer is in training, she can't waste her energy on silly games!"

"Sorry, Uncle Percy," said Penelope. "I guess I'll see you guys later," she said a little sadly, as her friends went off without her.

"In fact," said Uncle Percy, "I think it's time you were in your roost."

"But Uncle Percy," Penelope protested, "it's so early!"

"A Fancy Flyer needs her sleep, my dear!" said Uncle Percy. "Those wing muscles need lots of rest to get ready for all the work they have to do."

"Better do what Uncle Percy says," said Portia, as she helped Penelope settle on to her bedtime branch. "He's the expert!"

The next morning, Uncle Percy woke Penelope up very early.

"Time for your pre-dawn practice!" he squawked.

"But Uncle Percy, it's so early!" Penelope yawned. "The sun's not even up yet!"

"That's the best time to train!" said Uncle Percy. "Follow me!"

"We'll start with some speed exercises," Uncle Percy said. "They were my speciality when I was a Fancy Flyer. Just move in and out through the trees—like this!"

Penelope watched her Uncle weave gracefully through the jungle. It looked easy enough, but when she tried...

THUH-WHACK!

"Ouch!"
cried Penelope.

Uncle Percy came rushing back to look at
Penelope's head.

"Nothing serious," he said. "A Fancy Flyer in
training has to expect a few bumps and bruises!
Best thing to do is keep going. Let's try it again."

All day, Uncle Percy tried to teach Penelope stunts.
And all day, Penelope bashed...

...and crashed...

...and smashed...

...and splashed...

into trees, bushes, and other animals!

It was a very tired and worn-out Penelope, who headed for home with Uncle Percy that afternoon.

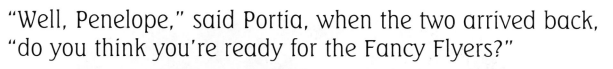

"Well, Penelope," said Portia, when the two arrived back, "do you think you're ready for the Fancy Flyers?"

"Oh, yes," said Penelope. "And I know *exactly* what my speciality will be!"

"What?" asked Portia and Uncle Percy together.

"Watching from the audience!" laughed
Penelope.

The End